His mouth twisted into ▮▮▮▮
'Are we still friends, Ne▮▮▮

'Of course we are,' she insis▮▮▮
best mate.'

Oh, hell.

Deep breaths, Nell. Take deep breaths. True, your
heart is thudding like it's about to explode, but don't
say anything rash—because if you've got this wrong,
if you've misunderstood him, you are going to look
really, really stupid.

'Jonah, I...' She moistened her lips. 'When you say
that you wish you were... Do you mean that you
wish...that you...that...?'

He put down his teacup. 'Nell, I've always been lousy
with words, so maybe...' He reached out and cupped
her face gently with his hand. 'Maybe this might make
it clearer?'

Oh, hell. Oh, double, triple hell. His eyes were dark,
and hot, and he wasn't doing anything, simply cupping
her cheek gently with his fingers, and she knew he was
giving her plenty of time to back away, plenty of time
to get to her feet. But she didn't want to back away, and
she didn't want to get to her feet.

'Nell?'

So much conveyed in one little word. So much implied,
and asked, and understood. And though a niggling
little voice whispered at the back of her mind that this
was a very bad idea, the hand cupping her cheek was
trembling, and she was trembling, and she wanted so
much to kiss him, to know what it would feel like.
So when his lips came slowly towards hers she leant
forward to meet them without any hesitation at all.

Maggie Kingsley says she can't remember a time when she didn't want to be a writer, but she put her dream on hold and decided to 'be sensible' and become a teacher instead. Five years at the chalk face was enough to convince her she wasn't cut out for it, and she 'escaped' to work for a major charity. Unfortunately—or fortunately!—a back injury ended her career, and when she and her family moved to a remote cottage in the north of Scotland it was her family who nagged her into attempting to make her dream a reality. Combining a love of romantic fiction with a knowledge of medicine gleaned from the many professionals in her family, Maggie says she can't now imagine ever being able to have so much fun legally doing anything else!

Recent titles by the same author:

THE GOOD FATHER
THE SURGEON'S MARRIAGE DEMAND

A CONSULTANT CLAIMS HIS BRIDE

BY
MAGGIE KINGSLEY

First published in Great Britain 2006
Paperback edition 2007
Harlequin Mills & Boon Limited,
Eton House, 18-24 Paradise Road, Richmond, Surrey TW9 1SR

© Maggie Kingsley 2006

ISBN-13: 978 0 263 85213 4
ISBN-10:   0 263 85213 X

Set in Times Roman 10 on 12 pt
03-0107-55499

Printed and bound in Spain
by Litografia Rosés, S.A., Barcelona

A CONSULTANT CLAIMS HIS BRIDE

CHAPTER ONE

SHE'D been dumped. No matter how hard Nell Sutherland stared at the email on her computer screen, she knew it wasn't going to change. She'd been dumped. And not in person, not even in a phone call or a letter, but in a sodding email sent to her at work.

I expect you've realised we've grown apart.

Well, actually, no, I hadn't realised that, Nell thought. In fact, it would have been kind of hard for me to know anything when I'm here in Glasgow, and you're in New York, and for the last six months you've ended all your phone calls with the words 'Love you—miss you.'

I've met a wonderful girl called Candy.

And what does that make me? Nell thought with a spurt of anger. You must have thought I was wonderful once, Brian, or you wouldn't have lived with me for a year, or suggested we get engaged before you went to the States. And what sort of name was Candy? Candy was sweets, not women. Unless, of course, the woman in question was eye-candy and she'd bet her next ward manager's pay cheque that Candy was.

'Nell, Tommy Moffat's blood test results are back from the lab.'

Nell minimised the email quickly, fixed a bright and perky 'all's right with my world' smile to her lips, and turned to face the neonatal intensive care unit secretary.

'Good news, or bad?' she said, and Fiona frowned.

'Frustrating would be a better word. Tommy doesn't have anaemia, or any sign of an infection, so it looks like you're back to square one.'

'Damn,' Nell muttered, taking the results the secretary was holding out to her. 'Jonah was sure his failure to thrive was due to another bout of sepsis. He's going to freak when he hears it's not.'

Jonah would. The specialist registrar had always been a dedicated doctor but since Gabriel Dalgleish, the consultant in charge of the neonatal intensive care unit at the Belfield Infirmary, had left him temporarily in charge of the unit while he was away on his honeymoon, Jonah's dedication to the babies had gone into overdrive.

'He's working too hard,' Fiona observed, as though she'd read Nell's mind. 'Can't you get him to relax or, better yet, find him somebody to relax with as you did for Gabriel?'

Nell laughed. She'd been as amazed as the rest of the staff to see their brusque and aloof consultant fall in love with her cousin Maddie, but finding somebody for Jonah Washington was another thing entirely.

'If I had a flat tyre, Jonah would be the first man I'd call,' she said. 'If I needed help moving some furniture, it would be Jonah I'd ask. He's my best friend next to my cousin Maddie, but…'

'But no wow factor,' Fiona finished for her, and Nell nodded.

Jonah was…well, Jonah was just Jonah. A six foot four inches, solid bear of a man with light brown hair, and dark brown eyes, he was a rock any sensible woman would want to cling to in a storm but he definitely had no wow factor.

Brian had the wow factor by the bucketful. Tall, blond, with deep blue eyes and a devastating smile, he'd arrived at the Belfield Infirmary two years ago as the new consultant in charge of the anaesthetics department. He'd also arrived with a reputation as a heartbreaker but as Nell had never for one second imagined he'd be interested in a girl who was five feet nine, with a figure even her best friends described as 'generous', she'd treated him casually, dismissively, only to be completely stunned when he'd asked her out.

I'll always be very fond of you, Nell, but it's better for us both to know now that it would never have worked out than for us to have got married and been unhappy.

Yes, but better for who, Brian? she wondered, feeling tears prick at the backs of her eyes.

She was the one who was going to have to tell everybody at the Belfield their engagement was off. She was the one who would have to endure the false sympathy, the pitying looks, the whispered comments of how they'd all known it wouldn't last, not a girl like her with a man like Brian, while he was safe in New York.

'Nell, are you OK?'

A slight frown was creasing Fiona's forehead and Nell forced her bright and chirpy smile back into place.

'Fine, absolutely fine,' she said, getting briskly to her feet. 'I'd better take these results along to Jonah and Bea. They've been stressing about them all morning.'

'It must be odd, watching someone else doing your old ward sister's job,' Fiona said, as she followed Nell out of her small office.

'It is,' Nell admitted, 'but Bea's settled in really well even if she will persist in calling me Sister Sutherland instead of Nell.'

'Apparently, the ward manager of her last NICU was a real stickler for protocol.'

'Then her last ward manager needed to get a life,' Nell declared. 'My main concern is the smooth running of the unit, not whether people call me by my surname or my first name.'

Fiona laughed. 'Yes, but, then, you've never been big on attitude, have you?'

She hadn't, and maybe that had been her mistake. Maybe if she'd insisted on going to New York with Brian, instead of meekly accepting his decision that she should stay in Scotland, none of this would have happened.

'It would be crazy for us both to uproot ourselves from the

Belfield Infirmary for just a year,' he'd said. 'I'm only going because it's a once-in-a-lifetime opportunity for me to see how an anaesthetics department works in the States. I know we'll miss one another but I'll be back in Glasgow before you know it.'

Except now he wouldn't. He would be staying in New York with Candy. Candy who was probably a petite and perfect size six, with gleaming white teeth and the kind of tumbling blonde hair that wouldn't look out of place in a shampoo commercial.

'Nell, are you sure you're OK?'

Fiona's eyes were curious now, speculative, and Nell hitched her smile up so high it was a wonder her face didn't crack.

'I've just got a bad attack of Monday morning winter blues, that's all.'

'Tell me about it,' Fiona said with feeling. 'I hate October. It's such a depressing, absolutely nothing sort of a month, isn't it? I wish it was Christmas. It will be George's first, you know.'

And, as the secretary babbled on about her baby son, Nell made polite noises and scarcely heard her.

Where had it all gone wrong? *How* had it all gone wrong? She loved Brian. She'd thought he loved her. He'd said he did. He'd even said he loved her curves, but he'd also never objected when she'd told him she was going on yet another diet. Maybe if she'd stuck to the diets. Maybe if she hadn't confessed to him that her blonde highlights were fake and she was actually a dull and mousy brown underneath. Maybe if...

'Is that Tommy Moffat's blood test results?'

Jonah Washington was walking down the corridor towards them and, as Fiona hurried back to her office, Nell handed him the results and waited for the explosion to come.

It did.

'If he's not anaemic, or caught another infection, then what the hell's wrong with him?' Jonah exclaimed, dragging his fingers through his straight brown hair, making it look even more unruly than usual. 'I know he was twelve weeks premature, but preemies normally gain weight quite quickly once we've stabilised them and yet his weight gain in the two weeks he's been in NICU has been minuscule.'

'At least he *is* putting on weight,' Nell declared. 'I know it's not been much, but eating is one of the most energy-consuming processes for any newborn and preemie's digestive tracts are often just not sufficiently developed to handle food even if it's through an IV line.'

'Bea wonders if he could have necrotising enterocolitis,' Jonah said as though she hadn't spoken. 'I know there's no sign of tension in his stomach or blood in his bowels—'

'Jonah, if Tommy had any damage to his intestines, it would have shown up on the X-rays,' Nell interrupted gently.

'Yes, but what if the X-ray equipment is faulty?'

'It's highly unlikely.'

'But what if it is?'

'Jonah.'

He stared at her silently for a moment, then his lips quirked. 'I'm overreacting, aren't I?'

'Just a bit,' she said, and he laughed.

'Good old Nell. What would I do without you to keep me grounded?'

Good old Nell. That was how everybody saw her. Good old Nell, always game for everything, when in reality she was sometimes so nervous at social events that she felt physically sick. Good old Nell, who made jokes about her height and her weight but only to prevent other people making them first. How in the world was she ever going to get Brian back? And she did want him back. Desperately.

'Nell, is there something wrong?' Jonah said, his brown eyes suddenly concerned, and she managed a shaky laugh.

'You're the second person to ask me that this morning, and I'm fine. Just suffering from a bad attack of ward manager's paperwork blues.'

'You're sure that's all it is?' he pressed, and she felt a betraying flush of colour creep across her cheeks.

Hellfire and damnation. Jonah always seemed to sense when something was wrong with her, but she didn't want to tell him about Brian. Not yet, at any rate. Not when she was so perilously close to tears.

'Of course I'm sure,' she insisted. 'You've seen my office, Jonah. I'm drowning under forms and requisition sheets in there.'

For a moment she didn't think he believed her, then, to her relief, he nodded.

'Snap. I always used to wonder why Gabriel was first into the unit and last to leave. Now I know.'

'But you're enjoying being temporary master of all you survey,' she said, and he grinned.

'I think everyone has a little bit of the dictator in them.'

'You, a dictator?' She laughed. 'Jonah, you're as soft as butter.'

'Says the girl who's a complete pushover,' he countered, and it was only with the greatest difficulty that she kept her smile in place.

'Do you want me to set up Tommy's tests again?' she said, deliberately changing the subject.

'I'd feel happier if we did,' he admitted. 'I know you think I'm panicking needlessly…'

'But your gut instinct says something's wrong,' she finished for him. 'OK, I'll reschedule the tests, but I'll bet you a fiver he's simply a slow developer.'

'You're on,' he said as he led the way into the special care section of the unit.

'I see Donna's mother is here again,' Nell murmured, noticing Mrs Harrison sitting beside her daughter's incubator.

'Mrs Harrison is always here.' Jonah sighed. 'I've tried telling her there's no cause for concern, that her daughter is only in Special because she developed jaundice after she was born. Could you have a word with her? I've done my best, but it's like talking to a brick wall.'

It was.

'But I have to stay with Donna,' Sheila Harrison protested when Nell voiced Jonah's concern. 'If I leave her she might… she might…'

'Sheila, jaundice isn't a life-threatening condition,' Nell declared. 'It's simply caused by bilirubin, a byproduct of the natural breakdown of blood cells, not being recycled back into the body by the liver as it should be. We're giving Donna extra fluids and light therapy, and her body is now eliminating the excess bilirubin so we should be able to transfer her to Transitional quite soon.'

'Yes, but—'

'You have a boy of six and a girl of four, don't you?' Nell interrupted, and Sheila nodded.

'My mother's looking after them. She's been great.'

'I'm sure she has, but she's not your children's mum, is she? Sheila, tell me something,' Nell continued when the woman said nothing. 'How much time have you spent with your son and daughter since Donna was born?'

Sheila looked at her as though she was insane. 'Sister, my baby's lying here ill, and you're asking me how how much time I've…I've…'

'Been out enjoying yourself?' Nell finished for her. 'Sheila, you mustn't neglect your other children because Donna has to stay in the unit for a little while. If you do, they're going to resent her before you've even take her home.'

'But—'

'You need to spend time with them, and you need to take care of yourself,' Nell continued. 'Even if all you do is go for a walk, or read a book for an hour, it will relax you, make you less stressed, and the less stressed you are the better you'll be able to cope.'

'I guess so,' Sheila said uncertainly, then tears filled her eyes. 'It wasn't supposed to be like this, Sister. I thought I'd just take Donna home after she was born, like I did with my other kids, but life—it has a horrible habit of slapping you in the face sometimes, doesn't it?'

Tell me about it, Nell thought as she gave Mrs Harrison's shoulder a reassuring squeeze before walking towards the unit door. That morning, when she'd got up she'd thought she had it all. A fiancé, her new promotion to ward manager of the neonatal intensive care unit of the Belfield Infirmary, and now...

Now nobody's eyes would light up any more when they saw her. Nobody would make her feel loved, and special, the way Brian had.

'Nell?'

Jonah looked apologetic and her heart sank.

'Tell me the worst,' she said.

'Admin want a word about your patient through-put figures, the rep from the pharmaceutical company has just arrived, and Maternity are querying your transfer documentation for Adam Thornton.'

'What's there to query?' she protested. 'Adam was born in Maternity on Saturday. He developed breathing problems on Sunday and they transferred him down to us.'

'Apparently you didn't complete the form in triplicate. Sorry, Nell,' Jonah added as she groaned. 'It looks like it's going to be one of those days.'

He didn't know the half of it, she thought, but, then, neither did she. It turned out to be a nightmare Monday. Everything that could go wrong did go wrong. One of the ward nurses dropped Tommy Moffat's new blood samples just after they'd been taken, Bea screwed up the time the ophthalmologist was supposed to arrive to check Donna Harrison's eyes, the pharmaceutical rep overstayed his welcome by a good hour, and as for Admin...

'I tell you, Fiona,' Nell said as she shut the drawer of her filing cabinet with a bang. 'If Admin had phoned me one more time today I would have—'

'Marched down to the second floor and rammed the phone down their throats?' the departmental secretary suggested, and Nell shook her head grimly.

'I was thinking of somewhere considerably more painful.' She glanced at the clock on her office wall. 'Lord, is it half past eight already? I'm off home for a bath, and a mindless evening spent curled up on the sofa in front of the TV.'

'But you can't,' Fiona protested. 'We're all supposed to be going down to the function suite after we finish our shifts. For Wendy's leaving bash, remember?'

Nell hadn't remembered, and now she'd been reminded she didn't want to go. Wendy might be a lovely girl, and terrific at hurrying up their test results when they sent them down to Urology, but she was leaving because she was pregnant. Which meant tonight's event would be dominated by jokes about bumps and stomach-churning Oh-my-God-but-I-thought-I-was-being-torn-in-two stories, and she didn't want to listen to either.

'Fiona, I'm sorry, but—'

'Jonah, tell Nell there's no way she can duck out of Wendy's farewell buffet,' Fiona interrupted, as the specialist registrar appeared at Nell's office door. 'We're all expected, aren't we?'

'Nobody is going to notice if I'm not there,' Nell protested. 'I'm so tired, and by the time I go home, get changed—'

'You don't need to change,' Jonah declared. 'Just take off your uniform and put on what you came into work in. That's what I'm going to do.'

Yes, but I bet you didn't come into work wearing your oldest denim shirt and tatty jogging trousers, Jonah.

'We're not going to take no for an answer, Nell,' Jonah continued as she opened her mouth to say just that. 'And I bet you anything, you'll have a ball.'

He'd been wrong, Nell thought, an hour later as she stood rammed up against the wall of the function suite unable to move because of the crush of people around her. An hour spent having her bikini line waxed would have been infinitely preferable to listening to everybody enjoying themselves while she felt as though her heart was breaking.

Tears welled in her eyes and she sniffed them back. Lord, but she was getting maudlin now, and she hadn't even had that much to drink. Just two glasses of wine because Jonah still hadn't returned from the scrum around the bar with another one for her.

'What are you doing hiding away in this corner?' Liz Fenton, the sister from obs and gynae, demanded as she pushed her way through the throng towards her. 'You're usually right out there in the middle of everything.'

'Rough day, Liz,' Nell muttered, trying to sidestep her colleague without success.

'Fiona was telling me Maddie and Gabriel are in Sweden at the moment, then they're off to Philadelphia and Boston, before coming back to Glasgow via Rome.'

Nell nodded. 'They'll be away for six weeks in all.'

'Nice for some,' Liz said dryly. 'My honeymoon was two weeks in Inverness. It rained every day.'

'Be fair, Liz, Gabriel's never taken all of his annual leave,' Nell protested. 'And he's using part of his honeymoon to check out all the new developments in neonatal care in Europe and the States.'

'Poor Maddie.' Liz laughed. 'I hope you've told Brian you've no intention of spending any of your honeymoon visiting anaesthetic departments.'

I want to go home, Nell thought. *I just want to go home.*

'Wendy looks radiant, doesn't she?' Liz continued. 'Have you and Brian decided whether you're going to try for a baby right away after you're married, or wait for a bit?'

'If she's any sense, she'll wait,' Fiona said, appearing at their side. 'Not that I'd ever be without George, but when I remember all the stitches I needed after he was born. Maternity said…'

Get me out of here, Nell thought as Fiona launched into a wince-inducing account of how George's head had been so big he'd torn her vagina in two places. *Somebody—anybody— please, get me out of here.*

'Maybe I should help Jonah with our drinks,' she said quickly. 'It's so crowded in here.'

Liz groaned. 'Oh, hell, Patty's crying again.'

'Patty?' Nell repeated. 'Who's Patty?'

'Patty Burton, one of the radiology technicians. Her boy-friend dumped her at the weekend.'

Nell glanced in the direction of Liz's gaze and saw a girl in a tiny, figure-hugging black dress, sobbing into a handkerchief. *Know how you feel, Patty.* Well, she didn't know how it felt to wear a tiny, figure-hugging black dress, but she did know all about the being dumped part.

'Maybe one of us should go over, see if we can help?' Nell said uncertainly, and Liz shook her head.

'Not unless you want her to listen to her repeat "But I love him" for the rest of the evening.'

'Maybe she does,' Nell protested. 'And if she does, she must be feeling awful.'

'Agreed.' Fiona nodded. 'But walking around like a wet lettuce isn't going to get him back, is it? What she needs is to start dating somebody else, make her rat-fink ex-boyfriend jealous, let him see what he's missing.'

Which was fine in theory, Nell thought, except the world wasn't exactly overflowing with eligible, fanciable men.

'I know it must be tough if you've picked a jerk,' Liz observed, 'but there's lots of good men out there. Look at my Sandy.'

Nell preferred not to. No man who was obsessed with rare chicken breeds could ever light her fire.

'Or Fiona's Graham, or your Brian, Nell,' Liz continued. 'Loyal, dependable, every one of them. And speaking of Brian,' the obs and gynae sister continued, 'you must be missing him like crazy.'

'I...I'm sorry, but you'll have to excuse me,' Nell said desperately. 'I've just seen...'

Nobody. She'd seen nobody, but she had to get away or Wendy's leaving bash was going to have two sobbing members of staff as a sideshow.

'Hey, no need to panic,' Jonah said, his smile broadening as she elbowed her way through the crush of people in front of her only to walk straight into him. 'I've got your drink.'

'Give it to Liz or Fiona,' she said. 'I'm leaving.'

'But the party's hardly started,' he protested, and she shook her head.

'It's over as far as I'm concerned.'

'Oh, come on!' he exclaimed. 'It's not like you to walk out on a slap-up buffet.'

His brown eyes were dancing and suddenly it was all too much for her—Brian's email, her rotten day—and something inside her snapped.

'You mean I'm a big fat pig who would go anywhere she could stuff her face,' she retorted. 'Well, thanks, Jonah. Thanks for nothing.'

The laughter in his eyes died instantly.

'I didn't say that,' he protested. 'I would never even think it. Look, what's the matter with you? You've been stretched tighter than a wire all day.'

'Why does there have to be anything the matter with me?' she demanded, trying to push past him, but it was like trying to move a boulder. 'Why do I always have to be happy Nell? Can't I ever feel down, or miserable, or…or just plain fed up?' Oh, Lord, if she didn't get out of there soon she was going to burst into tears. 'Get out of my way, Jonah.'

'Not until you tell me what's wrong,' he said.

'Jonah, if you don't get out of my way, I swear I'll stomp on your foot.'

He thrust the glass of wine he was holding into the hands of a startled passing junior doctor, then folded his arms over his chest. 'Stomp away, Nell, because I'm not moving.'

He meant it. She could tell from the look on his face that he meant it, but she could also see concern on his features, concern and kindness, and the tears she'd been trying so hard to keep in check all day filled her eyes.

'Take me home, Jonah,' she said, her voice breaking. 'Please. I just want to go home.'

Well, she'd done it now, she thought, seeing his eyes narrow. He was going to want to know why she was in such a state, but to her amazement he didn't say anything. Not when he tucked his arm under hers and created a pathway for them towards the door. Not even when they travelled down together in the elevator or walked out of the hospital.

'I'm sorry for shouting at you,' she said with difficulty when they reached his car. 'It was wrong of me, and I apologise.'

'Nell, you don't need to apologise to me,' he said. 'I obviously said something that upset you.'

'You didn't. Honestly, you didn't.' *Tell* him. Tell him what's happened. But she couldn't. 'Can we go now?' she said instead, and after a moment's hesitation he nodded.

To her relief they drove in silence to her flat, but from the sidelong glances he kept giving her she knew it was only a temporary respite and, sure enough, when he drew his car to a halt, and she reached for the passenger door, he put out his hand to stay her.

'Can I come in?' he said. 'Just for a minute?'

Part of her wanted to say no, that she was tired, that she didn't want to answer the questions she knew he was going to ask, but the other part also knew she didn't want be alone in her flat, surrounded by memories of Brian. She didn't want to spend the rest of the night wondering how she'd screwed up, why he'd found somebody else when he'd said-he'd *sworn*-he loved her, and so she nodded.

'Can I get you something to drink?' she said after she'd unlocked her front door and ushered Jonah into her sitting room. 'I've tea, coffee, or there's a couple of bottles of wine in the fridge.'

'A coffee would be good.'

He could have whatever he wanted just as long as he didn't go, she thought as she went into her kitchen, switched on the percolator, then opened the fridge.

'Are you sure about the coffee?' she said, carrying one of the bottles of wine into the sitting room. 'It won't take a minute but I thought I'd try some of this. It's supposed to be very good.'

Leastways, Brian had said it was when he bought it, and as he was never going to drink it now...

'I'll stick with coffee as I'm driving,' he said, but as he watched her open the wine and pour herself a liberal glassful, a frown pleated his forehead. 'Nell, I've known you for two years and this isn't like you. Something's clearly upset you and I want to know what it is.'

He wanted to know what it was. Fine, she would give him part of it.

'My hair...' She reached up and touched her short, straight bob self-consciously. 'Jonah, the blonde highlights are fake.'

'And very nice they look, too,' he said with a smile as he sat down on the sofa.

'Jonah, did you hear what I said?' she said in exasperation. 'My natural hair colour is brown. Plain, ordinary, mousy brown. The blonde highlights are fake.'

The frown on his forehead reappeared. 'And what's that got to do with anything? My sisters change their hair colour so frequently I have to ask them for an update before they visit otherwise I'd never recognise them.'

'There's more,' she said, downing her wine in one gulp. 'I was thirty-two last month, Jonah. *Thirty-two*.'

He looked even more puzzled. 'And I'll be thirty-six next February. So what?'

'It doesn't matter for you,' she said, sitting down in the armchair opposite him and topping up her glass. 'You're a man. No matter how old and wrinkly you get, everyone will simply say you're mature. I'm a woman and people are soon going to be calling me an old bat.'

He smothered a laugh. 'Nell, I hardly think being thirty-two makes you an old ba—'

'Jonah, I'm a thirty-two-year-old, fat, five-foot-nine inch female with dyed hair and boring grey eyes.'

'No, you're not,' he protested. 'Your hair is lovely, your eyes are beautiful, and you're not fat. You're statuesque, curvy.'

'I'm fat, Jonah,' she interrupted, 'and do you want to know something? I *hate* the way I look. I want to be a size six instead of a size sixteen. I keep going on diets, but...' she waved her hand expansively, sending part of the wine in her glass sloshing onto the carpet '...they don't work, and you know why they don't work? Because I cheat. I end up so damned hungry I cheat.'

'Nell, there is nothing wrong with the way you look,' Jonah declared. 'You're fine just as you are.'

Tears welled in her eyes and she sniffed them back. 'You're a good friend, Jonah, a good mate. Are you sure you don't want some of this wine? It really is very good.'

'You obviously think it is,' he said dryly as he watched her empty her glass, 'but I'm driving, remember? Look, why don't you phone Brian? I know he's going to be back in six months, but you're obviously missing him.'

'He's not coming back.' There, she'd finally said it, and now she had his full attention.

'You mean he's staying in the States?' he said slowly. 'You're going out there to join him?'

'No, I'm not going out there to join him. He...he's found somebody else. This...' She stared down at her engagement ring for a second, then pulled it off and put it down on the coffee-table. 'I shouldn't be wearing this because he doesn't want to marry me any more. He wants to marry somebody called Candy, and I...I...'

She couldn't say any more, and Jonah looked hard at her as she reached for the bottle of wine again.

'I think you've had enough of that.'

'It beats slashing my wrists,' she said, striving to sound flippant, but Jonah didn't seem to find it amusing.

He got to his feet, pulled the wine bottle out of her hand and set it down on the coffee-table beside her engagement ring with a clatter.

'Don't ever let me hear you say that again,' he said, his eyes icy. 'Not even as a joke. OK, so Brian has found somebody else, but these things happen. Relationships fail—'

'And I just have to pick myself up and start all over again,' she finished for him tartly. 'Well, that's just dandy, Jonah. That's just swell, and I'm sure in a few months' time I'll be able to think like that, but right now I can't, OK?'

'So you're going to drink yourself into a stupor for the next few months,' he said as she reached for the bottle again.

'Sounds good to me,' she said, and under Jonah's disapproving gaze she defiantly poured herself another glass and gulped it down.

Actually, she could see now why people got drunk. Your vision became a little blurry, and your head might not feel as though it was completely connected to your body, but it warmed you, relaxed you. In fact, she was so relaxed that Jonah's disapproval suddenly seemed funny and she started to giggle.

'Nell, you've definitely had enough to drink!' he exclaimed, and she stuck her tongue out at him.

'Oh, for God's sake, lighten up, Jonah,' she said, leaning back in her seat and missing the arm of the chair by a mile.

'Nell.'

She sighed. 'All right, all right. If you're going to be boring, I'll get us both coffee.'

And she fully intended to do just that, but when she stood up a rush of blood suddenly sped from her legs to her head and before she knew what was happening she'd pitched forward onto the carpet, missing the coffee-table by inches.

'Nell, are you all right?'

Jonah's voice was anxious, tense, and she rolled over onto her back and stared fuzzily up at him.

'Of course I'm all right. Except what are you doing up there while I'm down here?'

He shook his head. 'I think it's time you were in bed,' he said, and she fluttered her eyelashes at him.

'Ooh, Jonah, that's the best offer I've had in ages.'

With a sigh he reached to help her up, and she waited for him to put his back out when he tried to lift her, but he didn't. Never before had she felt small and fragile, but somehow Jonah managed to make her feel both as he lifted her effortlessly up into his arms.

'My hero.' She hiccuped as he carried her out of the sitting room. 'Superman in a white coat. Where are you taking me, Mr Superman?'

'To your bedroom, if I knew where it was,' he said.

'Second door on the right,' she replied, waving an unsteady hand down the hall. 'You know, you have lovely hair, Jonah,' she added, nuzzling her nose into the side of his neck. 'I never realised you had such lovely hair. Soft, silky. Smells nice, too.'

'Don't do that, Nell.'

His voice sounded strained, constricted, and she tickled the hair at the nape of his neck with her fingers and giggled.

'Why not? It's nice. You're nice.' He muttered something she didn't catch, and she planted a kiss at the base of his throat, only to feel him jerk his head away. 'You're my knight in shining armour, Jonah. My true-blue, always-there knight in shining armour.'

A knight in shining armour who was going to leave, she suddenly realised when they reached her bedroom and Jonah gently began to lower her onto her bed. But she didn't want him to leave. She didn't want to lie there all alone, remembering she'd been dumped. She wanted to feel desired, attractive, and before she could rationalise her thoughts, or Jonah could straighten up, she flung her arms around his neck and pulled him down on top of her.

'Nell, what the…?'

'Stay, Jonah,' she whispered. 'Stay with me.'

He shook his head, his face unreadable. 'Nell, you don't know what you're saying.'

'I do,' she insisted. 'I do. Don't go. I don't want you to go.'

And as he opened his mouth, clearly intending to protest, her lips met his and silenced him.

CHAPTER TWO

IT WAS the insistent ringing of her alarm clock that woke Nell with a start. A ringing that went straight through her skull with all the force of a dentist's drill.

Gingerly, she tried to sit up, only to lie down again swiftly with a groan as the contents of her stomach lurched up into her throat. She'd never been a drinker and now she remembered why. Two glasses of wine were her limit and she couldn't begin to count how many she'd had last night. Too many, if her throbbing head and churning stomach were anything to go by.

With an effort she turned on her side, and froze. Two aspirins and a glass of water were sitting on her bedside cabinet. Two aspirins and a glass of water she knew she hadn't put there yesterday.

Jonah.

'Oh, God, tell me I didn't,' she whispered, squeezing her eyes shut as memories of last night began creeping into her mind. 'Tell me what I'm thinking happened didn't happen, and it was just a bad dream.'

But it wasn't. When she lifted her duvet she could see she was still wearing her bra and knickers. At least it was her halfway decent bra and knickers, as opposed to some of her threadbare and tatty underwear, but that didn't alter the fact that she was still

wearing them. That Jonah had taken one look at her all too cur-
vaceous curves and decided he wasn't interested.

A sob rose in her throat and she put her hand to her mouth to
quell it. If there was one thing more humiliating than waking up
after a drunken one-night stand, it was waking up to remember
that the man you'd thrown yourself at had rejected you.

And she had thrown herself at him. Her brain might be fuzzy
but it wasn't fuzzy enough for her to forget that it had been she
who had dragged Jonah down on top of her when he'd lowered
her onto her bed. She who had pulled off her shirt and trousers
despite his best efforts to prevent her, and she who had kept repeating, 'Make love to me, Jonah. I want you to make love to
me,' before she'd passed out.

Oh, God.

On the Richter scale of embarrassment it was worse than
coming out of the loo not realising you'd tucked your skirt into
your knickers. Worse even than asking the man you'd been dating
for a while whether your relationship had moved into commitment
and realising from the stunned look on his face that it hadn't.

How was she ever going to be able to face him? For two years
they'd been such good friends. They'd laughed together, com-
miserated with each other, and once she'd even cried on his
shoulder after a really bad day, but now... In the space of twenty-
four hours she'd not only been dumped by her fiancé she'd also
made a complete and utter fool of herself with the one man who
had always been there for her in the good times and the bad.

A tear rolled down her cheek and she brushed it away angrily.
She'd got herself into this mess, and somehow she had to get
herself out of it.

'I was drunk, Jonah, and didn't know what I was doing,' she
said out loud, then shook her head, wincing as she did so.

That was insulting. So insulting.

'Brian had dumped me, and I needed to feel wanted, and I
knew you wouldn't hurt me, so I...'

Worse, that was worse. Neither his pride nor their friendship would survive that amount of honesty.

Somehow she had to come up with a convincing explanation for her behaviour, but *what*?

Right, Nell thought, taking a deep breath as the elevator doors opened onto the fourth floor of the Belfield Infirmary. It's plan A. You don't refer to last night and Jonah will think you don't remember it, and because he's a gentleman he won't remind you. End of story.

It sounded good. Sort of. At least it was better than plan B.

'Hey, what happened to you last night?' Fiona called as Nell tried to sneak past her office. 'One minute you were in the function suite with Liz and me, and the next you were gone.'

'I was feeling a bit rough so I decided to go home,' Nell muttered, and Fiona frowned at her.

'You still don't look very great,' she observed, 'but it was a terrific party, wasn't it?'

'The best.' Nell lied, feeling the dentist's drill inside her head beginning to intensify. 'Is…is Jonah in?'

'Arrived about half an hour ago. Full of beans, too.'

Full of beans.

Did that mean he was laughing at her, laughing at what she'd done? No, of course Jonah wouldn't laugh. He wasn't the type. Or at least she didn't think he was.

'He left a message for you,' Fiona continued. 'Said he'd like a word some time today.'

That didn't sound good.

'Did he say what he wanted to talk about?' Nell asked, determinedly casual, and Fiona shook her head.

'Maybe he's still worried about Tommy Moffat.'

That sounded better. Well, not better for little Tommy, but definitely better for her.

'Jonah's in Intensive at the moment if you want to see him

before you start your shift,' Fiona continued helpfully, and Nell managed a weak smile.

She didn't want to see Jonah. She wanted a couple of mugs of black, unsweetened coffee before she went anywhere near the specialist registrar or the unit, but she'd no sooner reached her office than Bea appeared.

'One newbie admitted at three o'clock,' the ward sister said, holding out the night staff's notes to her. 'Katie Kelly, ten and a half weeks premature, mum and dad's names are Tricia and Rob.'

'Anything else?' Nell asked, gazing longingly at the jar of coffee on her desk and knowing she had as much chance of grabbing a cup as she had of suddenly changing into a five foot nothing, size six film star.

'Tommy Moffat. Jonah said his BP was all over the place last night.'

Nell's hand faltered as she reached for her uniform. 'Jonah was in the unit last night?'

'He said he had nothing better to do so he thought he'd pop in.'

Oh, ouch, there was only so much honesty a woman wanted to hear, even if it came secondhand.

'Increase the frequency of Tommy's obs,' Nell said with difficulty. 'If his BP keeps on fluctuating, let me know immediately.'

Bea nodded. 'Are we still transferring Chloe Wilson and Winston Turner from Special to Transitional today?'

'Both have been breathing without their ventilators for the past month, and they're also feeding well with no reflux action so—'

'They're almost ready to go home.' Bea smiled. 'Don't you just love being able to tell parents that? It's what makes working in the NICU so worthwhile.'

It was. Nell knew that some nurses, and quite a few doctors, found the unit unnerving but she had always loved her work. The challenge of keeping the tiny preemies alive, the relief when they started to grow, the joy when they finally left the unit to go home with their parents. Of course, it wasn't always like that. There were dark days, grim days, when one of their tiny charges lost their hold on life, but she had never wanted to work anywhere else.

Except today, she realised, after she'd changed into her uniform and Bea led the way into the intensive care section of the unit and she saw Jonah deep in conversation with Callum Nicolson's mother.

'Viv's a bit upset because she still hasn't been able to express any milk to feed her son,' Bea murmured as they saw Jonah put his arm around Mrs Nicolson and give her a hug, 'but he's good in these situations, isn't he?'

He was. A lot of doctors possessed the necessary skills to make them proficient neonatologists, but to be a really good one you needed to be able to put yourself into other people's shoes, to empathise with them, and Jonah could do that with his eyes shut. He was also unexpectedly good at fending off the advances of drunken women, but Nell didn't want to think about that right now.

'Is that Rob and Tricia Kelly?' she asked, seeing a couple she didn't know standing awkwardly by one of the incubators.

Bea nodded. 'Jonah's explained we're going to have to take it one day at a time, but I think they're still a bit shell-shocked.'

Nell would have been shell-shocked, too, if one minute she and her husband had been happily asleep in bed and the next she'd gone into labour ten and a half weeks prematurely.

'This place—it's a bit overwhelming, isn't it?' Rob said, when Nell walked over to the couple to introduce herself

'There's nothing to be frightened of, truly, there isn't,' Nell said. 'Your daughter's really just in a kind of mini-greenhouse, which will keep her warm and cosy until she's well enough to cope with the outside world.'

'But all those wires, all those tubes,' Tricia said, twisting her dressing-gown belt round in her fingers, her voice uneven. 'It looks so painful.'

'Katie needs help with her breathing and feeding, Tricia,' Nell said gently. 'We also need to keep an eye on her heart rate and blood pressure. Do you see the monitor up there?' she continued, pointing to the screen above the incubator. 'All of Katie's wires and tubes are linked to it so we can see at a glance how she's doing.'

She could also see that Jonah was still talking to Callum Nicolson's mother. Was it her imagination or was he avoiding looking in her direction? No, he was looking at her. Actually, he was staring at her. Probably thinking, *Streuth, but that uniform sure hides a multitude of sins*.

Stop it, she told herself, just stop it. It's plan A, remember? You don't remember last night. Just keep telling yourself that, and maybe you'll start to believe it.

'Sister?'

Tricia Kelly was gazing at her, her eyes very bright, and to Nell's horror she realised the woman had obviously just asked her something, but she didn't have a clue what it was. Lord, but now she wasn't just a drunken slut, she was also completely unprofessional as well.

'I'm sorry, Tricia,' she said, her cheeks darkening. 'I didn't quite catch…?'

'I just said I wish I could hold her,' Tricia replied. 'If I could hold her, I'd feel…I'd feel she was more mine.'

'You'll be able to hold her in a few days,' Nell said, pulling herself together quickly. 'At the moment we just want to ensure she's stabilised, plus—'

'Plus it can be quite stressful for babies to be touched if they've never been held before,' Jonah chipped in as he joined them. 'Which, of course, they haven't because they've been safely cocooned in their mumies' tummies.'

Tricia managed a smile. 'But won't I dislodge all those tubes and wires when I'm allowed to hold her?'

Jonah shook his head. 'They're all firmly attached and in a few days you won't even notice them. You'll be holding and kissing your daughter without a second's thought.'

He'd kissed her last night, Nell remembered. Or rather, she'd kissed him. Just the once and then he'd wrenched his head away, muttering something unprintable under his breath. It had been a nice kiss, though. Actually, it had been more than nice. It had been…

Unconsciously she shook her head. Booze really screwed up your reasoning powers because, just for a moment when she'd kissed him, she'd felt really odd. Sort of tingly, expectant, almost—

'Nell?'

Oh, damnation. Now Jonah had obviously asked her something and she didn't know what that was either. She really was going to have to pull herself together or it wouldn't be just last night she'd have to worry about. It would be whether she still had a job.

'It's Viv Nicolson,' Jonah murmured, stepping out of earshot of the Kellys. 'She's having real problems with the breast pump. I've told her the milk will come, but…' his brown eyes crinkled '…I'm at a bit of a disadvantage with not possessing any of the necessary equipment myself, so I wondered if you could have a word, woman to woman.'

'You know, some people might consider that a very sexist remark,' she replied, trying and failing to prevent her lips from curving, and he laughed.

'Guilty as charged, but in this case it's true.'

'Yes, but just because I have breasts doesn't mean I automatically know how to use a breast pump,' she began, only to immediately wish she hadn't. Talking about breasts to a man who had seen a lot of hers than he'd probably ever wanted to was not a good idea. 'I mean…I can try…I'll do my best.'

And before he could say anything else, she shot off in Viv Nicolson's direction, determined to lose herself in her work.

It didn't help. Nothing helped as the day dragged by. No matter what she did, whether it was trying to reassure Viv that even if she never mastered the breast pump it didn't matter because formula milk was just as good, or supervising the transfer of Chloe Wilson and Winston Turner to Transitional Care, she knew her mind was only half on her job. One glimpse of Jonah was enough to make her heart slide down into her stomach, and every time he spoke to her she knew she was analysing what he said, looking for hidden references, subtle innuendos.

She was going to go mad if she tried to stick to plan A. It would have to be plan B. Plan B which involved coming clean and apologizing, no matter how toe-curlingly embarrassing it was.

'Yikes, but you look even worse now than you did when you first came in this morning,' Fiona observed, when Nell handed her the notes for the night staff. 'If I were you, I'd go straight home and have an early night.'

'I fully intend to,' Nell replied. 'I just want a quick word with Jonah. Is he about?'

'He was in his consulting room a few minutes ago, but I'm not sure where he is now.' The secretary stared at Nell critically. 'You know, you could be coming down with flu. Liz Fenton was telling me last night—'

'Got to go, Fiona,' Nell interrupted, before the secretary could launch into a long and involved saga on who in the nursing staff was currently laid low with what.

Get it over with, she told herself as she headed off down the corridor. Grovel profusely, and get it over with—but not right away, she realised with dismay as she rounded the corner and saw her least favourite member of staff walking towards her.

'And where are you hurrying off to at such speed, not so little Nell?' Lawrence Summers, the consultant from Men's Surgical, said with one of his aren't-I-wonderful smiles. 'Not so little Nell, as opposed to *the* little Nell,' he added. 'Get it?'

'Very amusing, sir,' she muttered. 'And now if you'll excuse me,' she continued, but he moved faster than she did and blocked her path.

'It's Lawrence, Nell, as I keep telling you,' he said. 'Not sir, or Mr Summers, but Lawrence. And what's your hurry? Stay a while, talk to me.'

Yeah, right, she thought. The only reason you want to talk to me is so you can ogle my breasts. So, maybe she was more than generously endowed, but every time she met the consultant it was getting harder and harder to resist the temptation to wrench up his chin and say, 'Look, I'm more than just a pair of breasts, just as I'm sure you're more than what you've got in your trousers.'

Except she wasn't one hundred per cent certain that Lawrence actually was more than what he had in his trousers.

Brian had loathed him.

'Flash beggar,' he'd said one evening when they'd been having dinner. 'Getting by on his good looks and so-called charm. I've worked with him in Theatre, Nell, and, believe me, he's all show and no substance. One day he'll come a cropper.'

Nell didn't know whether the consultant would or not, but she did know she didn't want to be ogled by him.

'I'm afraid I have to go, Mr Summers,' she said firmly, but before she could push past him he had caught her hand.

'When are you going to go out with me, Nell?'

When hell freezes over, Lawrence. 'I'm an engaged woman, sir.'

'An engaged woman who isn't wearing her engagement ring,' he said, lifting her hand into the light and regarding it thoughtfully.

Oh, damn and blast. She'd forgotten to put it back on again after last night, and though she knew she'd have to eventually tell everyone about her broken engagement, Lawrence was the last person on that particular list.

'It's in the jeweller's,' she said quickly. 'I…I noticed one of the stones was loose this morning so I left it with the jeweller to be on the safe side.'

One of Lawrence's eyebrows rose. 'Why do I have the feeling you're lying?'

'Perhaps because you have an overly suspicious nature?' Jonah said as he came out of his consulting room. He glanced from Lawrence to Nell, then back again. 'You also appear to be manhandling a member of my staff.'

His voice was even but Nell could hear the hint of steel beneath it, and so, apparently, could Lawrence because he released her hand immediately.

'No offence meant, Nell,' he said. She knew he expected her to reply, 'None taken,' but she would have cut out her own tongue than say it.

'So, what brings you up from the rarefied atmosphere of Men's Surgical, Lawrence?' Jonah asked, and the consultant smiled.

'Haematology tell me you've been complaining about the length of time you're having to wait before they test any samples you send down, and I thought I should point out to you, as one member of staff to another, that we all have to follow a certain protocol.'

'The protocol being that Men's Surgical samples should always be tested first, and the rest of us have to wait in line,' Jonah said, with a smile every bit as false as Lawrence Summers's. 'I don't think so, Lawrence.'

'Then perhaps I should also point out that you're only an acting consultant,' Lawrence continued, his smile completely gone now, 'and therefore have no real authority to insist on anything.'

'Feel free to point out whatever you like, Lawrence,' Jonah said smoothly, 'but it won't get you anywhere.'

The two men stared at one another, and Nell held her breath. Only yesterday she'd told Jonah he was as soft as butter, but this was a Jonah she didn't know. A Jonah she wouldn't want to mess with. Lawrence clearly thought the same.

'Fair enough, Jonah,' he said, his smile back in place on his handsome face. 'I just thought I'd mention it.'

'I'm glad you did,' Jonah replied. 'And now, if you'll excuse us?' he added pointedly, which left Lawrence with nothing to do but leave.

'Thanks for rescuing me,' Nell said as she followed Jonah into his consulting room. 'That man is such a creep.'

'Lawrence Summers is a creep?' Jonah said in surprise. 'I thought he was God's gift to women?'

'In his dreams,' Nell retorted. 'He may look like a Greek god but anyone who's ever been out with him says he's got arms like an octopus and a kiss like a bathroom plunger.'

Jonah let out a splutter of laughter. 'That's an image that's going to stay with me for a very long time. Now, what can I do for you?'

'Do for me?' she said, momentarily confused, and his eyes crinkled.

'Well, as you were clearly headed for my room before you were waylaid by the dreaded Lawrence, I assume you wanted to speak to me.'

She did, but now she was here…

Say it, she told herself. The longer she didn't say it, the harder it was going to be. Which was true, but it didn't make the prospect of raising the subject of last night any easier.

'Jonah—' She came to a halt as his phone rang.

'I'll be with you in a minute,' he said, lifting the phone, only to roll his eyes in exasperation at whatever the person at the other end of the phone was saying. 'No, I do not *want* the results tomorrow,' he told the unknown caller. 'I want them today. They were promised for today, and this is today, so where are they?'

He winked across at her, and she tried to smile back, but as she stood uncertainly in front of his desk, words crept into her mind. Words that made her cheeks heat up, and her resolve falter.

You have such lovely hair, Jonah. Soft, silky. Smells nice, too.

Oh, criminy, had she really said that? Maybe she should forget all about plan B and go back to plan A.

'Would you believe that Haematology still haven't processed Donna Harrison's blood tests?' Jonah said when he'd put down the phone. 'I told them I need to be sure her jaundice has completely gone before we can discharge her.' He dragged his fingers through his hair then smiled a little ruefully. 'Enough with the complaining. What can I do for you?'

She opened her mouth, then closed it again. 'It doesn't matter You're clearly busy, and it's not important.'

'It obviously is, otherwise you wouldn't be standing there looking like you've got your knickers in a twist.'

Knickers. He'd seen her knickers and they weren't frilly or pretty but the sort of serviceable, practical kind his mother probably wore.

Oh, for heaven's sake, stop thinking about your knickers, her mind urged. Just say it because if you don't you'll only have to try again tomorrow and that will be even worse.

'It's…it's about what happened last night, Jonah,' she said and his eyes met hers.

'Nothing happened last night, Nell.'

'I know nothing happened in the sense of…of *happened*,' she said, wishing she was anywhere but there, and doing anything but having this conversation, 'but that's only because…because you were too much of a gentleman to take advantage of the situation.' *Or took one look at me and thought, ye gods, but I hadn't realised she was quite that fat.*

'That's true,' he said solemnly, then one corner of his mouth lifted. 'Plus I have this rather old-fashioned notion that if I make love to a woman, I rather prefer her to be able to remember it afterwards.'

'Oh. Right.' She could feel a blush creeping all the way up from her toes. 'Jonah.'

'Look, you were unhappy last night, and very drunk,' he continued. 'Nothing happened you need be embarrassed about.'

Oh, yes, it had.

'And as far as I'm concerned, the subject is over, forgotten My only regret is that Brian isn't standing in front of me righ now. He's behaved very badly, and if he were here I'd take the greatest pleasure in inflicting some serious damage on him.'

'You would?' she said in surprise, and he shook his head as though amazed she should doubt it.

'Nell, we're friends, and I won't allow anyone to make a friend of mine unhappy.'

Tears rose in her throat and she gulped them back with difficulty. 'You're the best, Jonah. You know that, don't you?'

'I think the words you used last night were "my hero", "Mr Superman" and "my knight in shining armour".'

Crimson colour seeped across her cheeks and she gave an unsteady laugh. 'I thought you said you'd forgotten all about last night?'

He grinned. 'I have, but I kind of liked those descriptions so, if you don't mind, I'd like to remember them.'

She tried to keep her smile in place, but it wobbled around the edges, and he got to his feet and clasped her hands in his own large ones.

'Brian's an idiot,' he said softly. 'This Candy, you're worth two of her.'

'I bet I weigh two of her as well,' she said miserably, and he tilted her chin with his finger.

'Enough of that. Nell, listen to me—'

'Jonah, I've been thinking about Brian…what's happened… It's partly my fault, isn't it?'

'Your fault?' he repeated. 'How the hell can it be your fault?'

'I should have gone to the States with him. I know he said there was no point in me going with him as it was only for a year, but Brian likes company, and I think he was lonely, living in a city he doesn't know. And this Candy…she's been there, somebody for him to talk to, and before he realised what was happening, she grabbed him.'

'Bu—'

'It makes sense, doesn't it?' she said. 'And, if I'm right, there's still a chance he'll realise he's made a mistake and come back to me, isn't there?'

Her grey eyes were large and dark as she stared up at him, and it took all of Jonah's self-control not to shake her.

How could she be so trusting, so gullible, so damned *stupid*? he wondered. Brian was, and always had been, an arrogant, conceited jerk. In fact, Jonah had been more surprised that the anaesthetist had stayed faithful to Nell for as long as he had than the news that he'd dumped her.

Then tell her so, his mind urged, but, having grown up with five sisters, Jonah knew only too well that the last thing a woman wanted to hear on an occasion like this was the truth.

'I suppose it's possible,' he said vaguely, and felt his heart twist inside him when a blinding smile illuminated Nell's face. A smile he knew wasn't meant for him but for Brian.

Lord, but he wanted her. He always had, but when he'd first come to the Belfield he'd still been getting over a disastrous relationship that had left both his heart and his ego badly bruised. He'd decided to take it slowly, not to make the same mistake again, only to watch with dismay as Nell had fallen in love with Brian Weston. Once the engagement ring was on her finger she'd been off limits as far as he was concerned, but now...

'Nell—'

'I was wondering whether I ought to fly out to the States,' she interrupted. 'Talk to him?'

'Absolutely not,' he said firmly. *In fact, over my dead body.* 'You're both too raw emotionally at the moment, and I'm also going to have to be rather selfish here...' *And to lie through my teeth if necessary.* '...and point out that with Gabriel away on his honeymoon, the unit really couldn't manage if another member of staff went on leave.'

'No, of course not.' She sighed, then smiled awkwardly. 'I'm just sorry I made such a complete fool of myself last night, embarrassing you the way I did.'

'You didn't embarrass me,' he declared, and she hadn't.

When he'd seen her in all her lush, creamy glory, felt her breasts straining against him as she'd lain beneath him, it hadn't been embarrassment he'd felt, it had been desire. A burning, overwhelming desire, and only the knowledge that she had been drunk had prevented him from tearing off the remainder of her clothes and burying himself deep inside her.

'Like I said, it's forgotten,' he said lightly. 'But what I don't want is you going back to your flat every night and drinking yourself into oblivion.'

She shook her head. 'I'm never doing that again. I thought I was dying when I woke up this morning.'

He laughed. 'What you need is to get out of your flat in the evenings. Maybe go out for a meal with some friends, or perhaps just one particular friend.'

Like him.

'But if Brian heard I was going out, he might think I didn't love him any more,' she protested.

Good, Jonah thought, because for the past two years I've been calling you 'good old Nell' in an attempt to desexualise you, but now your engagement is off I'm going to do whatever it takes to win you.

'Or it could bring him to his senses, make him fly over here.' He lied.

'I suppose,' she said, clearly unconvinced, then her eyes filled with tears. 'I want him back, Jonah. I just want him back.'

And I want you, he thought, but he had no illusions about himself. He was too big, too ordinary, to be any woman's idea of a wonderful catch, but if he let Nell's wounds heal for a couple of months, gave her time to realise and accept that Brian wasn't coming back, then maybe, just maybe, he might have a chance.

'Jonah?'

She was staring at him uncertainly and he realised he was frowning and quickly smoothed out his face.

'It's time you went home,' he said. 'You look exhausted.'

She felt it, but to go home to her empty flat…

'I thought I might stay on for a while, catch up on some paperwork.'

'Go home, Nell, and that's an order,' he said, and she gazed up at him quizzically.

'An order?' she said, and he smiled.

'I can be very determined when I want to be, Nell.'

Unexpectedly so, she thought with wry amusement as he steered her out of his consulting room towards the elevators but, then again, perhaps not. She'd always suspected there were parts of Jonah she didn't know. Parts he kept well hidden.

She knew he was a terrific friend. She also knew he was hopeless with women. Three months was the longest she'd ever known him date anybody and it wasn't because he was a serial flirt. His relationships just seemed to peter out with no hard feelings on either side.

Maybe she should try that, she thought when she got home and a hard lump formed in her throat when she saw so many of Brian's belongings lying where he'd left them. Dating just for fun and then moving on without regret. But how could she move on when it was still Brian she wanted?

A tear trickled down her cheek and desperately she picked up the magazine she'd bought in the newsagent's on the way home and flicked through it, only to stop when her eyes fell on the title of an article: *Tired of always being dumped by your boyfriends? Then stop being reactive!*

'And what the heck's reactive?' she muttered aloud, kicking off her shoes, curling up on the sofa and reading on. '"Proactive people make things happen. Reactive people sit back and let things happen to them."'

Well, that was her in a nutshell. A reactive wimp, a reactive doormat. Somehow she had to become a proactive person, but how? Fiona had said last night that the girl from Radiology needed to show her ex-boyfriend she didn't care. Even Jonah had said Brian might come back if he heard she was going out, enjoying herself.

She sat up straighter on the sofa. What if she started dating again, even just for a couple of dates? Brian had lots of friends at the Belfield and one of them would be sure to email or phone him. If he heard she was dating again, it might remind him of what they'd shared, make him jealous, get him to fly back to Glasgow. And once he was here, who knew what might happen?

Yeah, right, she thought, her optimism subsiding, and just who was she going to date? The Belfield isn't exactly chock-a-block with single, fanciable men, plus you'd have to explain to this man that the dates weren't real, only a means to an end.

Jonah. Jonah would do it in a minute, but Brian would never be jealous of Jonah.

'He's a nice enough bloke, Nell,' Brian had said once, 'but he's never going to amount to anything, is he?'

It had been the one and only time they'd had a row, but having a row about Jonah wasn't enough. She'd have to date someone he could see as a rival. Somebody handsome. Somebody who would get right under his skin. Somebody like….

Lawrence Summers.

The consultant was always asking her out, and she wouldn't have to tell him why she was suddenly saying yes after months of saying no because he had a hide like a rhinoceros. Admittedly, he was a groper and a creep, but she could handle him, she knew she could.

A triumphant smile curved her lips. Lawrence Summers. Lawrence Summers would be perfect.

CHAPTER THREE

'IT'S not that I'm hurt, or offended, or anything,' Fiona said, the tightness around her mouth indicating she most certainly was, 'but to hear your engagement was off from someone like Lawrence Summers…'

Nell gritted her teeth. It had taken just fourteen hours for the blabbermouth consultant to ensure that the rumour had spread right around the hospital. If she hadn't needed him for a date she would have marched straight down to Men's Surgical and kicked him smack in the middle of his ego.

'My engagement isn't off, Fiona,' she replied as calmly as she could. Well, it wouldn't be off if her plan worked, and she was going to do her damnedest to make sure that it did work. 'Brian and I have simply decided we need a little breathing space, that's all.'

Disbelief was written all over Fiona's face, and it had been the same with everyone Nell had met that morning. From the porters in Reception to the clutch of nurses who had all but hijacked her on her way up in the elevator, everyone had looked at her with either a 'Brian's a sleaze ball and you're well out of it' expression or a barely disguised and infuriatingly smug 'Well, I knew it would never last' one.

'Fiona—'

'I'm a bit busy at the moment, Nell,' the secretary interrupted. 'So, if you'll excuse me…'

Terrific, just terrific, Nell thought as Fiona stomped into her office and slammed the door. She'd known that she couldn't keep her broken engagement a secret for ever, but she'd at least hoped for a little longer than forty-eight hours to get her emotions under control, and now Fiona was in a huff because she hadn't confided in her first.

'Adam Thornton had to be transferred from Special into Intensive last night,' Bea said when Nell reached her own office. 'He developed serious breathing problems just after midnight.'

'How many breaths a minute?' Nell asked, pulling on her uniform.

'More than sixty. I was wondering about transient tachypnoea of the newborn but he's more than forty-eight hours old now so it's not likely, is it?'

Nell shook her head. 'I would have said RSD but, like transient tachypnoea, respiratory disease syndrome usually affects preemies, not full-termers. Pneumonia perhaps, or a blood infection?'

'Your guess is as good as mine,' Bea said, and Nell shook her head wryly.

'You'd better not let any of the parents of our babies hear you saying that.' She clipped her name tag to her collar and slipped a stethoscope into her pocket. 'How's Tommy this morning?'

'His temperature went up a little during the night, but it's back to normal again this morning, and Katie Kelly had a very good night.'

'Great,' Nell said with relief, and Bea nodded, then gazed at her a little uncertainly.

'I know it's none of my business but I just want to say how very sorry I was to hear about your engagement. I'm not going to say anything else,' the ward sister continued as Nell tried to interrupt, 'except I think he's a rat for treating you like this.'

Why am I the only one to see that Brian isn't a rat, that he'd simply got lonely? Nell wondered. OK, Jonah could see it, but one person amongst the four hundred staff at the Belfield was scarcely an overwhelming show of support.

Well, she would show them, she told herself as she strode down the corridor and into Intensive Care. She would make each and every one of them eat their sympathetic words.

'I hear this little one has a problem,' she said, as she joined Jonah at Adam Thornton's incubator.

'It's an odd one,' he replied. 'All his symptoms point to RDS, the fast and hard breaths, his skin and muscles pulling in each time he takes a breath, but he's a full-term baby not a preemie.'

'Could his mother have got her due date wrong?' Nell suggested. 'He was quite small at birth, just two and a half kilos, so perhaps he was actually born four to six weeks premature and nobody realised it.'

'It's certainly possible,' Jonah observed, 'and prematurity would mean he'd have the immature lungs conducive to RDS. Set up a chest X-ray for him, and give him artificial surfactant through his breathing tube. If it *is* RDS, the sooner we get on top of this the better.'

'Do his parents know he's been transferred into Intensive?'

'They came in last night,' Jonah said. 'I told them there's no immediate cause for concern, but you know what parents are like.'

She did. In fact, she'd lost count of the number of times mothers had cried their eyes out on Jonah's shoulder.

'Oh, and it looks like I owe you a fiver,' Jonah continued. 'Tommy Moffat's repeat sample results are back from the lab, and there's not a sign of an infection or any congenital abnormality.'

'Does that mean I get to say "I told you so" all day?' she said, her grey eyes sparkling, and he laughed.

'Absolutely. I'm never happier than when I'm proved wrong about a less than optimistic prognosis.'

Nell tilted her head and regarded him quizzically. 'Then why do I get the feeling you're still not one hundred per cent sure you *are* wrong?'

Jonah looked as though he was about to deny it, then sighed. 'Maybe I'm too emotionally involved because Tommy was the first baby to come under my care after Gabriel left on his honeymoon. Maybe I'm overcompensating because as an acting consultant I don't want anything to go wrong. Maybe—'

'You're just a very conscientious specialist registrar,' Nell finished for him. 'Bea's his primary carer, isn't she? How about if I tell her to flag up if he so much as turns over in his incubator?'

'I'd feel like I was making a mountain out of an mole hill.'

'Yes, but would it make you happier?' she insisted, and when, after a moment's hesitation, he nodded, she said, 'Then consider it done.'

'No bet that your specialist registrar is becoming a control freak with paranoid tendencies?' he said ruefully, and she laughed.

'Nah. I've picked up a lot of things myself by going with my gut instinct, so who am I to diss yours?'

'Speaking of gut instinct, I'd better warn you that Liz Fenton is on the loose,' Jonah said, as he and Nell walked across the unit together towards Katie's incubator.

'It's surely not time to buy tickets for the Christmas party already, is it?' Nell said, and Jonah shook his head as he retrieved Katie's clipboard and scanned it quickly.

'The committee has decided to host an extra fundraising event this year because they made such a loss with the spring car treasure hunt.'

'I'm not surprised,' Nell protested. 'Who, in their right mind, would want to race around Glasgow in the middle of the night in March, looking for clues?'

'I suppose it would depend on who you were with,' Jonah said, his eyes dancing, and Nell's heart clenched slightly.

He was right. The treasure hunt had been the last event she and Brian had taken part in before he'd left for the States, and they'd been so happy then, so very much in love.

And you will be again, her heart whispered, so enough of the moping, enough of the self-pity.

'What kind of extra event are they putting on?' she asked, determinedly bright.

'An amateur talent contest.'

Nell's mouth fell open. 'You're kidding.'

'Nope. You know, Katie really is doing very well,' he continued, replacing the clipboard. 'Her BP's stable, her heart rate's good and her breathing is excellent, considering how premature she was at birth. I don't want to be over-optimistic, but it's looking good.'

'And I don't want to be over-critical,' Nell declared, 'but surely if the committee is going to hold a talent contest, one of the essentials is having people with some talent willing to perform.'

'According to Liz, her husband Sandy plays all the classic symphonies on his harmonica.'

Nell pressed her lips together. 'That should make for a fun night out.'

'And Mr Portman is apparently more than willing to perform some magic tricks.'

'Andrew Portman from Orthopaedics?' she exclaimed. 'Jonah, he gets lost between his own department and the canteen.'

'In that case, I can't wait for him to perform his vanishing trick.'

For a second she managed to restrain herself, but only for a second.

'Oh, Jonah,' she whooped. 'I'm going to have to buy a ticket for this, if only for the unintentional comedy.'

'If it will help to make you laugh again, I'll insist they hold a talent contest every week,' he said softly, and she shook her head at him.

'Will you stop worrying about me? I'm fine, apart from the fact that the whole of the Belfield staff seems to know I'm not engaged any more.'

'I didn't say anything,' he said with alarm, and she put her hand on his arm and smiled.

'I know you didn't, but it doesn't really matter who started the rumour because I've been thinking about what you said. About it being a bad idea for me to sit about moping at home, so I've decided—'

'Sorry to interrupt,' Bea declared as she joined them, 'but Rob Kelly's in your consulting room, Jonah, and he'd like a word.'

An uncharacteristic look of irritation appeared on Jonah's face.

'OK, Bea, but don't think this means you're off the hook, Nell. I want to know what you've decided so no leaving the hospital tonight until you've told me, OK?'

Nell smiled as she watched him walk away. He was a good friend, a very good friend. In fact, if she possessed one whit of common sense she would have fallen in love with him instead of Brian but, then, as everyone knew when it came to falling in love, common sense went right out the window.

So, too, did all her plans to make some serious inroads into her paperwork. The agency nurse hired to cover the sick leave of one of the unit nurses didn't turn up and there was nothing Nell could do but take her place.

'I bet you never thought you'd be back in the unit, writing up obs again,' Bea said after lunch as they moved from incubator to incubator in Intensive Care.

'Strangely enough, it's this sort of hands-on work I miss most,' Nell replied. 'Though I have to admit I'd forgotten how much bending over there was.'

'There speaks a ward manager who's gone soft.' Bea chuckled, then flushed to the roots of her hair. 'I'm sorry. I shouldn't have said that, it was unforgivable.'

'No, it wasn't,' Nell protested. 'Look, will you relax?' she continued, as Bea stared at her, clearly mortified. 'I'm not an ogre, and working in this unit is so stressful at times that if we didn't share an occasional laugh we'd crack.'

'You and Jonah seemed to be enjoying a good laugh this

morning,' Bea observed. She shot her a swift sidelong glance. 'You like him, don't you?'

Nell smiled. 'Everyone likes Jonah.'

'He reminds me a little of my husband. He doesn't say much either, and men like that…' the ward sister shot her another speculative glance '…tend to get overlooked, don't they?'

Nell didn't see how anyone could possibly overlook Jonah. There was his height, for a start, and his broad shoulders, but she didn't say that.

'I think Jonah can stand up for himself,' she said instead.

'Yes, but…' Bea came to a halt. 'Megan Thornton's just arrived,' she murmured, 'and the poor woman looks as though she didn't get a wink of sleep last night. Do you want to speak to her, or will I?'

'I'll do it,' Nell declared, and was glad she'd volunteered when Megan Thornton promptly burst into tears the moment she saw her.

'I know Dr Washington said there was no cause for concern,' she sobbed. 'But Intensive Care. Babies aren't transferred here for nothing, are they?'

'Megan, please, don't upset yourself,' Nell said gently. 'Adam was just having a bit more trouble with his breathing last night so it was decided, just to be on the safe side, to move him into Intensive Care.'

'Yes, but…' Megan let out a shuddering breath and shook her head. 'I don't know whether I'm on my head or my heels, Sister. One minute I was in labour, then the next my son was transferred into Special Care, and now he's in Intensive Care, and everyone keeps telling me not to worry.'

'Megan, can I ask you something?' Nell interrupted. 'Is it possible you got your due date wrong? You see, Adam was very small when he was born,' she continued as the woman looked at her in confusion, 'and we were wondering whether he might, in fact, be an eight-month baby rather than a full-term one.'

'I suppose it's possible,' Megan said slowly. 'I never was

very regular, and I sort of guessed when my last proper period was. Is it important?'

'It could be,' Nell said. 'You see, when a full-term baby is born, the baby's body produces a chemical known as surfactant just after birth which enables the inner surface of his or her lungs to expand properly. Premature babies don't have enough surfactant in their lungs, so they develop something called respiratory distress syndrome.'

'And you think Adam might have that?'

'It's a possibility,' Nell said carefully. 'Dr Washington is going to X-ray Adam's lungs today, and that will confirm whether he has RDS or not.'

The girl smiled weakly. 'If it's not one thing it's another, isn't it, Sister?'

Nell smiled back.

'It can seem like that at times, but Adam's in the best possible place. Never forget that.'

'Nell, Liz is outside, and she'd like a quick word with you if you have time,' Bea murmured, after Megan had walked over to her son's incubator.

Nell didn't, but she also knew that if she didn't see Liz today, the obs and gynae sister would be back tomorrow and the day after.

'I'll be five minutes, Bea,' she said. And that's all she was going to be, she told herself when she went out into the corridor and saw Liz waiting for her, a clipboard in her hand and a look of determination on her face.

'Liz, if this is about the talent concert—'

'It is,' Liz interrupted, 'but before I bend your ear, I just want to say how very sorry I was to hear you and Brian have called off your engagement.'

Nell clenched her teeth together until they hurt. Maybe she ought to get a sign made saying she'd kill the next person who told her how sorry they were. Except, of course, everybody would then say she'd flipped, and that would give them even more to talk about

'Thanks, Liz, but I really don't want to discuss it,' she said and could tell from the disappointment on Liz's face that she'd been all set for a cosy chat. 'And you don't have to tell me anything about the talent contest,' she continued. 'Jonah's already put me in the picture, and I'll be more than happy to buy a ticket.

'I was rather hoping to persuade you to take part,' Liz said 'We're a bit short of volunteers, you see, and the big night's in two weeks time.'

'Two weeks?' Nell repeated. 'Isn't that a bit short notice?'

'It's not like the people taking part will need much time to rehearse,' Liz said. 'They'll all know what they're doing.'

Yeah, right. Like Andrew Portman knew anything about conjuring tricks.

'So, can I put you down for something?' the Liz continued 'Maybe singing a song, telling some joke——'

'Sorry, Liz,' Nell interrupted. 'I'll be there in the audience cheering everyone on, but as for taking part, singing in the bath is about as far as my performing ambitions go.'

The sister's face fell. 'Do you think Jonah might be interested?'

'You can certainly ask him,' Nell replied bracingly. 'And now if you'll excuse me…'

And before Liz could talk her into something she knew she would regret, Nell walked back into Intensive Care, shaking her head. A talent contest. Of all the dumb, guaranteed-to-be-a-complete-disaster ideas the committee could have come up with, this had to take the biscuit. The staff of the Belfield might be extremely dedicated and professional medical people, but performers?

She chuckled out loud. One thing was certain. She wouldn't miss it for the world.

She wouldn't have wanted to miss the beaming smile on Viv Nicolson's face either.

'Milk, Sister Nell!' the girl exclaimed, holding up a small

bottle. 'I've finally beaten the dreaded breast pump, and I wanted you to be the first person to know.'

'Oh, well done,' Nell said. 'Very well done, indeed.'

'I won't be able to feed him myself yet, though, will I?' Viv said regretfully. 'With a bottle, I mean.'

'I'm afraid not,' Nell replied. 'Babies born seven weeks prematurely can't nurse at the breast, but we can store your expressed milk and give it to Callum through a nasogastric tube.'

'I'm so proud of myself, Sister,' Viv continued. 'I know you said it didn't matter if I couldn't master the breast pump, but I really wanted to do it. Can you tell Dr Jonah I have? I wanted you to know first, but I want him to know, too.'

'Of course I'll tell Dr Jonah,' Nell replied.

'Tell me what?' a familiar voice said, and Nell turned with a smile.

'Viv has triumphed over the breast pump.'

'I told you that you could do it, didn't I?' Jonah said, his face breaking into a grin. 'If I had a bottle of champagne, I'd crack it open for you. Or, then again, perhaps not,' he added with a wink. 'We don't want young Callum becoming an early alcoholic.'

Viv laughed, and Nell smiled inwardly as she listened to Jonah explaining to the young mother how the nasogastric tube worked. He couldn't have been more pleased about Viv's news if Callum had been his own son. He ought to have children of his own. He'd make a terrific father, whereas Brian... It was odd, but though he liked children she couldn't for the life of her picture him playing with any.

'Something wrong?'

She looked up to see Jonah's eyes on her and quickly shook her head.

'Not a thing,' she said, and his eyes narrowed slightly.

'I think you need a restorative cup of coffee.'

'I don't have time,' she protested. 'Bea needs help with the obs.'

'Bea can manage for another fifteen minutes on her own,' he said, guiding her firmly out of Intensive Care.

'OK, but I want you to know this macho stuff doesn' normally work with me,' she declared. 'I'm only having a cup of coffee because I want one.'

His lips twitched. 'Fair enough. Are you still taking your black with no sugar?' he said as he strode into his consulting room and switched on the kettle. 'Or have you gone back to wha you really like, white with two sugars?'

'Black with no sugar, please,' she said. 'I'm on a diet again.'

He shook his head. 'How many times do I have to tell you that real men don't want to date a bag of bones?'

He could say it as often as he liked but it didn't alter the fact that everywhere she went she saw images of waif-like ac tresses and super-models dressed in size six outfits looking ab solutely gorgeous.

'Black, no sugar,' she repeated firmly.

'You won't be wanting one of these to go with your coffee then?' he said, opening a paper bag and slipping out two Danish pastries.

She looked longingly at them. 'What flavour did you get?'

'Apple with cinnamon and sultana.'

'Rat fink.'

He grinned. 'Live a little. Start your diet next week.'

She was tempted, sorely tempted, but if her plan worked, and Brian came back, the last thing she wanted was to be even fatter than when he'd gone away.

'No sale. I intend to be virtuous.'

'Your loss is my gain,' he said without rancour, taking two mugs down from the shelf at the side of his desk. 'By the way your chat yesterday with Sheila Harrison seems to have worked She popped in for about an hour this afternoon, and left withou having to be forcibly ejected.'

'To be fair, I can understand how worried she must have

been,' Nell said. 'There she was, expecting a completely normal delivery, and suddenly she was catapulted into NICU.'

'Agreed, but she was running herself ragged. Are you sure about the black with no sugar?' he continued as he unscrewed the lid from the coffee-jar. 'OK, OK,' he added when Nell gave him a hard stare. 'On your own kidneys be it. So, what's this decision you were talking about this morning?'

She pulled over a chair to his desk and sat down. 'I've decided to start dating again.'

He looked momentarily stunned, then his face lit up. 'That's terrific news, Nell. Obviously you don't want to rush into anything too heavy, perhaps get yourself caught up in a rebound situation, so what I would suggest—'

'You've misunderstood me, Jonah,' she interrupted, taking the coffee he was holding out to her. 'I'm not talking about proper dating.'

'There's another kind?' he said as he sat down, and she chuckled.

'There is, and actually it was you who gave me the idea.'

His hand stilled as he reached for his own coffee. 'What idea?'

'That if I dated somebody and Brian got to hear about it—and he will because he's got heaps of friends at the Belfield—he might, well, he might become jealous and…'

'You think he'll come rushing back to Glasgow?'

Disbelief was plain in his voice and her cheeks prickled with heat.

'You said he would,' she said in a small voice. 'You said you thought it was possible.'

For a moment he said nothing, then he took a sip of his coffee and gazed at her over the rim of his mug, his expression suddenly thoughtful. 'So I did. Of course, for it to work, you'd have to find somebody you could confide in, a friend perhaps, or else you'd simply be using them, and that wouldn't be fair.'

'I've already thought of that,' she declared, 'and I know the perfect person. Lawrence Summers.'

His mouth worked soundlessly for a moment, then he banged his mug down on his desk, sending tiny droplets of coffee spattering everywhere.

'*Are you out of your mind?*' he exclaimed. 'You told me yourself Lawrence had arms like an octopus and a kiss like a bathroom plunger, and now you're telling me you're seriously considering going out with him?'

'Jonah.'

'And what makes you think he'll ask you out anyway?' he continued furiously, and Nell rolled her eyes in exasperation.

'Because he's been asking me out at least once a week since I came to the Belfield, plus he undresses me with his eyes every time we meet.'

'Does he?' His face became grim. 'All the more reason for you not to go out with him. Nell, if you can't see this is a recipe for disaster,' he continued as she tried to interrupt, 'can't you at least see it's morally wrong?'

'How is it morally wrong?' she demanded. 'He wants to go out with me, so I'll go out with him.'

'You're using him, Nell, and people have feelings.'

'Lawrence doesn't. He's got such a thick skin you couldn't hurt him if your skewered him with a pitchfork.'

'Everyone has feelings, Nell.'

'All right, Lawrence has feelings,' she said. 'I'll go out with him a couple of times, then tell him very nicely that it isn't working.'

'And in the meantime, what if he wants more from you than just a goodnight kiss at the end of a date. What are you going to do then?' Jonah demanded. 'Lawrence must outweigh you by a good twenty-five kilos, and if he decides he wants payment for his nights out, I don't much fancy your chances of rebuffing him.'

She hadn't thought of that, but it was such a good plan that she refused to back down.

'Jonah, Lawrence might be a creep, but I hardly think he would try to force himself on me.'

'Nell—'

'And Brian isn't going to come back if he hears I'm dating somebody ordinary, somebody boring, somebody—'

'Like me.'

An oddly twisted smile had appeared on his lips, and she flushed scarlet. Oh, hell, she hadn't meant him to think that, but the trouble was he was right. Not that he was ordinary and boring, but that Brian considered him so.

'Jonah, it isn't that, truly it's not,' she said quickly, 'but Brian knows what good friends we are. That, well…there's nothing sexual between us and never could be.'

'I see.'

She didn't think he did because she had never seen him look so angry. She'd seen him furious when somebody had screwed up in the unit, had seen him livid when Admin had sent down yet more pointless forms, but this was different. This was like sitting in front of a simmering volcano and she wished with all her heart that she'd never started the conversation.

'Jonah, I did think of asking you to help me out,' she said. Well, she had. Sort of. In a way. 'But—'

'I'm afraid I couldn't have helped you out even if I'd wanted to,' he interrupted, his voice tight. 'My girlfriend wouldn't like it.'

'Your girlfriend?' She put down her mug of coffee. 'I didn't know you had a girlfriend. I mean, you never said,' she added swiftly, suddenly realising how awful that sounded. 'Who is she? How long have you been dating?'

'She doesn't work at the Belfield,' he replied, not meeting her eyes. 'We've been dating for quite a few weeks but we decided to keep it quiet because we wanted to see how things went before we went public.'

'Oh. Right.' She picked up her coffee and put it down again. 'But she's nice, you like her?'

'Strangely enough, not everybody dates people they detest,' he said dryly, and she flushed.

'OK, I asked for that, but *is* she nice?'

'She's terrific.'

'Oh. Good. I mean, I'm really pleased for you.'

And she was, she thought as she reached for her coffee again. The odd, numb feeling she was experiencing didn't mean she was jealous or anything silly like that. It just meant she was hurt because she'd thought she and Jonah shared everything, and to discover he'd been dating somebody for a while and not told her…

'So when are you going out with Lawrence?'

She blinked at the unexpectedness of his question. 'I hadn' thought that far ahead.'

'Don't you think you should?' he said leaning back in his seat an odd, almost watchful expression in his eyes. 'I'd strike while the iron's hot, if I were you.'

'There's no hurry.'

'What about a week on Saturday? You're off duty then and, i the grapevine is accurate, Lawrence works pretty flexible hours.

'Yes, but I'll need time to prepare,' she floundered. 'Perhaps even buy a new dress.'

Which was a bare-faced lie, because a tweed skirt, heavy woollen sweater and flat shoes was the only sensible outfit to wear if you were going out with a man whose sole interest in you was in getting inside your knickers.

'I don't see why you need to buy a new dress,' Jonah smoothly. 'If Lawrence is as keen as you say he is, he won't care if you turn up in your uniform.'

'No, but—'

'Why don't you go down to Men's Surgical when you finish your shift? Start the ball rolling.'

It was a sensible idea, but there was a calmness about Jonah's voice, almost an indifference, that she found infuriating.

'Jonah, just a minute ago you were blowing a fuse at the thought of me going out with Lawrence,' she protested, 'and now you're practically shoving me out the door with him.'

'I just thought if you truly think dating him will bring Brian back, the sooner you do it the better, don't you?'

'I suppose,' she muttered, and just for a second she could have sworn she saw a glimmer of a smile in Jonah's brown eyes. 'Are you making fun of me? Jonah, if you're making fun of me…'

'Of course I'm not,' he said, cradling his coffee in his hands and leaning further back in his seat. 'I wouldn't make fun of something as important as your future. And speaking of the future, where are you planning on going with Lawrence on your date?'

'I—I don't know,' she stammered. 'Maybe out for a meal or to the movies.'

'A meal would be good because if Lawrence is as much of a waste of space as you say he is, you'll have an escape route. The movies, though.' He shook his head. 'Far too dark and intimate, unless you want to get up close and personal. My girlfriend and I go to a lot of movies.'

'Really,' she said, trying and failing to keep the waspishness out of her voice.

'Oh, yes.' He nodded. 'Never see much of the films, of course.'

She supposed he meant he and his girlfriend spent all their time at the cinema halfway down one another's throats. Well, she could have done without knowing that.

'If I were you, I'd stick to a restaurant,' Jonah continued. 'The Casio Antonio is good, or if you really want to push the boat out what about La Bonne Auberge? My girlfriend and I have been there quite a few times, and it's never disappointed us.'

'I'll bear it in mind,' she said tightly.

She also wished he'd stop saying 'girlfriend' all the time. It wasn't that she was jealous of this unknown person—why on earth should she be?—but his constant repetition of the word 'girlfriend' was really getting on her nerves.

'Are you sure you don't want one of these Danish pastries?' he asked, biting into one with relish. 'They really are delicious.'

'I'll pass, thanks,' she replied. 'In fact, I'd better be going. It's not fair to leave Bea on her own.'

'But you've scarcely touched your coffee,' he protested as she got to her feet.

'I'm not thirsty any more,' she said, and as she swept out of his room, closing the door with slightly more force than was strictly necessary, a small smile curved his lips.

So she was annoyed about his girlfriend. That was interesting, more than interesting. True, annoyance wasn't in the same league as jealousy, but it was a start. At least it meant he'd managed to get her to sit up and notice he was a man instead of some asexual pal or friend.

Except he'd dug himself into a hole, a rather large one, because there was no girlfriend. He hadn't been out with anyone for months, and he didn't know what had made him say that he had.

Oh, get out of here. You know damn fine, his heart whispered. You thought, when Nell said she was thinking of dating again, that this was your big chance. That if you started as her 'pretend' boyfriend, you could then gradually win her over, and when she implied you wouldn't be convincing even as a pretend boyfriend, and she'd rather go out with Lawrence Summers instead, you saw red.

Which meant he now had two choices. He could come clean and admit he'd been lying, or he could maintain the pretence and see what happened.

Maintain the pretence, a little voice whispered at the back of his mind. *What do you have to lose?*

Nothing, he thought, except he'd have to find a girlfriend, and find one fast, because he couldn't get away with an imaginary one for long. He needed a real, living, breathing girlfriend. Someone he could mention in conversation. Someone he could even produce a photograph of, and someone—and this was the most important of all—who wouldn't ask too many awkward questions.

A frown creased his forehead as he went out into the corridor.

but as he walked towards the unit a slow smile began to creep across his face.

Mary-Anne.

Mary-Anne would be perfect. She'd been saying only last week that she hadn't seen him for a while, that she could do with hitting the Glasgow shops before the Christmas rush got into full swing. He'd telephone her tonight, ask if she'd like to come and stay with him for a while.

'You look in a good mood, Jonah,' Bea observed as he strode into Special Care. 'Won the lottery, have you?'

'Not yet, Bea.' He winked. 'But with any luck, I might just be about to.'

CHAPTER FOUR

'TALK about dark horses!' Fiona exclaimed, her eyes gleaming 'Did you know Jonah had a girlfriend?'

'He did mention it in passing last week,' Nell said tightly 'Now, about my referral letters…'

'Last week?' the secretary repeated. 'I would have expected you to have known about this Mary-Anne ages ago, with you and Jonah being such good friends.'

So would Nell, but not for one second would she ever have said so.

'Fiona, my referral letter.'

'I wonder what she's like, where she works? It's definitely not at the Belfield because Admin told me they've nobody called Mary-Anne on their books.'

'You asked?' Nell said, outraged, but Fiona didn't even blush

'Of course I asked. I thought he might be trying to pull a fast one, put us off the scent.'

Nell had wondered about that, too, but unlike Fiona she would never have asked Admin for the information, not least because she knew they wouldn't have given it to her.

'I hope we get to meet her soon,' the secretary continued 'Though I can understand Jonah wanting to keep her away from the hospital. You know what this place is like.'

Nell did, but somehow she didn't think the news that Jonah

Washington had a girlfriend would create quite the same stir as the considerably juicier item that she had been dumped. Or as much of a stir as dating Lawrence Summers was going to cause after tomorrow night.

'Fiona—'

'I hope it works out for him. He's not had much luck with women, has he? And he deserves to be happy.'

He did, Nell thought as Fiona hurried off to answer her phone. And she wanted him to be happy, of course she did, but she couldn't deny she was hurt. She'd thought they were friends. Dammit, she'd told him all about Brian, even confessed she wore a size sixteen, and that her blonde highlights were fake, yet he hadn't told her something as simple as the fact he was dating somebody, far less that it had been going on for weeks.

'Just the person I'm looking for,' Bea declared as Nell reached Intensive Care. 'Jonah wants to know whether you've managed to complete all the paperwork to authorise Callum Nicolson's move from Intensive into Special.'

'It's done,' Nell replied, and the ward sister sighed with relief. 'Viv's been dancing up and down like a kid on Christmas morning, and if there'd been a hiccup…'

'She would have been bereft.' Nell chuckled.

And she would. The young mother had been keeping her fingers crossed for days that her son might be moved into Special Care, and when Jonah had finally given her the thumbs-up yesterday Viv's shriek of delight must have been heard halfway across the hospital.

'Is Jonah in Intensive?' Nell asked.

Bea shook her head. 'He's having a word with Tricia Kelly in his consulting room, but he should be along shortly if you want to talk to him.'

Nell did. She would have liked it even better if she could have persuaded him to join her for coffee in her office. She'd scarcely seen him since last week, and when they met, something was different. Oh, he was pleasant as always, had been more than happy to stop and talk about their small patients, but something was different, something had changed, and she couldn't quite pinpoint what.

You're overreacting, Nell, she told herself as she followed Bea down the corridor. *Seeing things that aren't there. Jonah's just overworked and you... You're stressed about your date tomorrow with Lawrence. Correction. You're not stressed. You've got a mega attack of cold feet.*

'It's really sweet, the way Jonah keeps talking about Mary-Anne, isn't it?' Bea said, breaking into her thoughts.

Nell didn't think it was sweet. In fact, Jonah's constant repetition of the words 'Mary-Anne says' or 'Mary-Anne thinks' was beginning to set her teeth on edge.

'He brought in a photograph of her this morning,' Bea continued. 'It's on his desk.'

I am not *going to ask*, Nell told herself. *I am not the sort of superficial and shallow person who judges other people by how they look, so I'm not going to ask.*

But she did.

'What's she like?'

'Tall, like Jonah, with gorgeous long curly brown hair, and very pretty.'

Very pretty.

Well, that was good. She was pleased that Mary-Anne was pretty with gorgeous curly hair. Delighted that Jonah had finally found somebody after so many of his relationships had fizzled out, and if she suddenly felt snarky it had absolutely nothing to do with the fact that Mary-Anne was an apparent paragon of perfection. It was simply because she hadn't slept well last night, hadn't been sleeping well for the past week.

'Helen Moffat looks a bit down,' Nell declared, deliberately changing the subject as she followed Bea into Intensive Care and saw Tommy's mother standing by her son's incubator.

Bea frowned. 'She's been like that for the last couple of days. I've asked if there's anything wrong, something that might be worrying her, but she insists she's fine. Maybe you can get more out of her.'

Nell did. It wasn't easy. It took a lot of coaxing, a lot of gentle probing, but eventually she persuaded Helen to reveal what was wrong.

'I think I'm an unnatural mother, Sister,' Helen said, her voice low, desperate.

'What in the world makes you think that?' Nell exclaimed. 'You're here every day, helping us to care for Tommy—'

'No, I'm not,' Helen interrupted. 'You, Dr Jonah, the other nurses, the machines—you do everything. I just sit here knowing there's nothing I can do, or say, that can help him or alter anything.'

'Helen—'

'When Ian and I first saw him…' Helen took a shuddering breath '…he looked so tiny, so frail, and we knew it was only the tubes and wires that were keeping him alive. We thought he would die that first night, that he wouldn't be there when we came in to see him in the morning, but…'

'But?' Nell prompted, as tears began to trickle slowly down Helen's cheeks.

'He didn't die, and so my husband and I started to hope, to believe that one day we would be able to take him home, but, Sister, I dread coming into the unit. If I can get into the unit without meeting Dr Jonah then I know Tommy's had a good night, but if Dr Jonah's there, waiting for me, it means something else has happened, something else is wrong.'

'Helen, I know it's difficult,' Nell said, reaching out and clasping the young woman's hands in her own. 'With preemies it's always two steps forward, one step back.'

'It's more than that, Sister,' Helen interrupted. 'Now it's like…it's like I can't feel anything any more. I come in to visit him, to sit and talk to him, and I know I love him, that it would break my heart if he died, but mostly I just sit beside his incubator feeling numb, like I'm here but I'm not here.'

'Helen—'

'There's something wrong with me, isn't there?' Helen exclaimed. 'I'm an unnatural mother, an unfit mother.'

'Of course you're not,' Nell declared. 'What you're feeling is perfectly normal. You've been through so much since your son was born. The shock of his birth, the fear that he wouldn't survive the night, and then the roller-coaster days that followed. And it *is* a roller-coaster.'

'But I should be able to *feel*,' Helen said. 'Where have all my feelings gone?'

'They're still there, Helen,' a deep voice said softly, and Nell turned to see Jonah standing behind her. 'The semi-detached feelings you're experiencing are your brain's way of coping with the situation. Nobody can exist in a permanent state of fear, they'd crack up if they tried, so your brain is suppressing your emotions to help you to survive. It doesn't mean you don't care, and it most certainly doesn't make you an unfit mother.'

'It doesn't?' Helen said uncertainly, and Jonah smiled at her.

'Helen, if I needed a mother, you'd be the first person I'd choose.'

She gave an unsteady laugh. 'How in the world have you ever managed to remain single, Dr Jonah?'

One corner of his mouth turned up. 'I guess I'm what my old granny used to call an unclaimed blessing, Helen.'

He was, too, Nell thought as she watched Jonah put his arms round Helen and give her a hug. Oh, he wasn't drop-dead gorgeous, but he had other qualities, terrific qualities that even she had to admit she'd taken for granted. Mary-Anne obviously hadn't and she really hoped she and Jonah would be as happy as she and Brian had been. OK, so that was a rotten analogy as she and Brian weren't together any more, but they would be. She was sure about that.

'Could you ask Bea to keep an eye on Helen, maybe call in the hospital chaplain to speak to her?' Jonah murmured, as he and Nell left the unit. 'She's obviously getting close to the edge, and the last thing we want is her collapsing under the strain.'

Nell nodded. 'I can't imagine what it must be like to be the mother of a preemie, never knowing what you're going to face from one day to the next.'

'Actually, it would be worse for us,' Jonah observed. 'We know too much.'

It was true, they did. No doctor could attempt to spare them worry by using complicated words and Latin phrases. Not that she and Jonah would ever have a baby, of course, because he had Mary-Anne, and it was Brian she wanted, plus if they ever did have one the chances were that it would inherit both their heights, and her weight, and end up resembling the Incredible Hulk.

'I wish I could wave a magic wand and make Tommy grow,' Jonah continued, breaking into her thoughts. 'I know he's had various infections, and problems with his breathing, but that's par for the course with preemies. It's his lack of growth that's worrying me.'

'Neither Helen nor her husband are very tall,' Nell observed. 'Maybe he's just going to be short.'

'Yes, but there's short and there's short,' Jonah replied. 'I've been wondering whether it could be pancreatic infantilism or achondroplasia, but he doesn't match any of the symptoms.'

'Would dwarfism show up at such an early age?' Nell said, and Jonah sighed as he came to a halt in the middle of the corridor.

'I doubt it, but I'm clutching at straws here, Nell. Something is wrong, I know it, feel it, but every bloody test we've performed has returned a negative.'

He looked tired and stressed and instinctively she put her hand on his arm. 'You'll figure it out. I know you will.'

He looked down at her hand with an oddly lopsided smile.

'Good old Nell,' he began, then shook his head. 'No, not good old Nell. To begin with you're not old, and...'

'And?' she prompted, and he opened his mouth, then

snapped it shut on whatever he'd been about to say and set off down the corridor.

'I forgot to ask you to start collating the discharge papers for Donna Harrison,' he said over his shoulder. 'She's doing well in Transitional, with no recurrence of her jaundice, so I'm looking to discharge her next week.'

Collating the paperwork was no problem, Nell thought, hurrying after him, but what she really wanted was to know what he'd been about to say before he'd clearly thought better of it.

'Jonah, what you said about me…'

'I'm not happy about Adam Thornton still being on the ventilator. I know we've established he definitely has RDS, but the longer we help him with his breathing the more likelihood there is of him developing bronchopulmonary dysplasia.'

Nell gave up. 'Do you want to put him on steroids? That would prevent any lung scarring from the oxygen.'

'I'd rather not go down that road if possible—the side effects from steroids…' He shook his head as he led the way into his consulting room. 'We'll keep him on the extra oxygen with diuretics for the moment, but if he still needs the ventilator after another week, we'll have a rethink.'

'Katie Kelly's BP is still rather low,' Nell began, only to pause when her eyes fell on his desk. Bea had said he'd brought in a photograph of Mary-Anne but, sheesh, she'd expected something small, discreet, and the damn thing was enormous, A4 size at least.

'Nell?'

She dragged her gaze away from the photograph and back to him. 'Yes?'

'Katie Kelly's BP.'

'I…um…' What was she saying about Katie's blood pressure? Oh, yes, now she remembered. 'We've increased her fluid intake, but I think she needs medication.'

'OK, I'll write it up. It's a good picture, isn't it?' Jonah continued as her eyes strayed back to the photograph on his desk.

'Of course, it doesn't do her justice but, then, photographs never do, do they?'

Mine certainly don't, Nell thought sourly. In fact, I always cut them up because I can't believe I look that bad.

'She's very pretty,' she said.

He beamed. 'Isn't she? And she has a terrific sense of humour. We laugh all the time when we're out together.'

Bet that's fun for the people sitting close to you.

No, that was childish and petty, and she wasn't going to be petty when Jonah was so clearly taken with the woman, but she was going to ask him something. Not something big, or deep, but suddenly she felt a bit awkward, which was odd because he'd never made her feel awkward before.

'Jonah, I…I was wondering whether you might like to come round to my place tonight for a meal? Just as a friend, of course,' she continued quickly, seeing his eyebrows rise. 'I know you and Mary-Anne are an item, but it seems ages since we had a good chat, and…well…I thought it might be nice.'

'I'm afraid I can't,' he replied. 'I'm rehearsing for the talent contest this evening.'

Nell blinked. 'You're taking part in the contest?'

'Didn't I tell you?' He frowned slightly. 'It must have slipped my mind.'

Yeah, right. Like having a girlfriend had also somehow slipped his mind. They were supposed to be friends and yet increasingly it was beginning to feel as though the friendship was a one-way street.

'What are you doing in the contest?' she asked as calmly as she could.

'Three friends and I formed a band back in med school. We enjoyed it so much we kept it going. We're never going to be stars, but we do get the occasional booking for wedding receptions and charity gigs.'

Which meant he was virtually semi-professional. Virtually

semi-professional and in a relationship. What else didn't she know about him? That he'd been married and divorced six times, had four children and was hiding out in Glasgow from the Mafia?

Overreaction, Nell, a little voice whispered in the back of her mind. *Mega overreaction. You and Jonah aren't joined at the hip. He doesn't have to tell you everything about himself.*

No, but being in a band and having a girlfriend are pretty big omissions, she told the little voice angrily.

'What sort of music do you play?' she asked, willing herself to sound interested instead of aggrieved.

'A bit of rock and roll, a few ballads, stuff like that.'

Rock and roll? Good grief, she doubted whether anybody under the age of thirty would even recognise the term and those who did would think Jonah and his three friends positively pre-historic. Or they might laugh, and she couldn't bear it if people laughed at him. He was much too nice for that.

'Jonah, much as I like rock and roll—' actually, she didn't '—I don't know whether many other people will.'

'It'll be fun.'

As long as it was fun rather than funny, she thought, but he was a grown man, and there was nothing she could do but be there on the night to give him moral support and flatten anybody who so much as sniggered.

'Have you got everything arranged for tomorrow night?' he continued.

'Tomorrow night?' she repeated, her mind still grappling with the unlikely mental image of Jonah as a rock and roll singer. 'Oh, my date with Lawrence. Yes, it's all arranged.'

'You were right, then, about him being eager to go out with you?'

She'd been more than right. One trip down to Men's Surgical with the top button of her uniform undone and Lawrence had been all over her like a dog in heat.

'Yes. Yes, I was right,' she said, suddenly realising Jonah was waiting for her to reply.

'Good. Good.' He shuffled the files on his desk as though he was looking for something. 'Are you going somewhere nice?'

'La Bonne Auberge,' she replied. 'Apparently, it's one of Lawrence's favourite restaurants so he's booked a table for eight o'clock.'

'Good. Good,' he repeated, then glanced at his watch. 'Well, if there's nothing else, Nell, I am rather busy.'

She looked completely taken aback, and he wasn't surprised. He'd never been brusque with her, wouldn't have believed less than a fortnight ago that he ever could be, but brusqueness was part of his plan and he had to stick to it if he was to have any chance of success.

'Oh. Right,' she murmured. She half turned to go, then paused. 'Jonah?'

Oh, hell, don't look at me like that, he thought, quickly picking up one of the files from his desk to prevent himself from reaching for her, and giving her a hug.

'Hmm?' he said, deliberately vague.

'I just…'

Lord, she looked so woebegone, so hurt, but he couldn't back down now, and it wasn't just because he'd look such a fool after he'd spent the whole week babbling about Mary-Anne. It was because he couldn't forget Nell's implication that he was too boring, too ordinary to even qualify as a temporary boyfriend. That had hurt. That had hurt big time, so he flicked open the file and stared down at it as though it was the most scintillating thing he'd ever read.

'You just what?' he asked.

'It doesn't matter,' she mumbled. 'I…I'm sorry to have disturbed you.'

You've always disturbed me, he thought, keeping his eyes firmly fixed on the file until the soft click of his door told him she'd gone. Disturbed my mind, disturbed my dreams, but never did you realise it, not once.

He sighed as he sat down at his desk, and let the file in his hands slip from his fingers. Maybe it was all his own fault. Maybe he should never have allowed himself to become Nell's confidant, the listener to her worries, the giver of advice when she was in trouble, but, pathetic though it might be, having just that tiny bit of her had been better than not having anything of her at all.

Now he knew it wasn't enough. It never had been, and he'd been fooling himself to think it was. He wanted more. He wanted her, and if this plan didn't work, he'd cut his losses and start applying for specialist registrar posts at other hospitals.

But not just yet, he thought as his gaze fell on the photograph on his desk. He'd seen how often Nell's eyes had strayed to it, and perhaps after tomorrow night...

Which reminded him. He had a phone call to make, an important one, and a smile tugged at the corners of his mouth as he reached for his phone.

On Saturday night Nell decided she had lost what little sanity she'd ever possessed when an obsequious waiter seated her and Lawrence at one of the secluded tables in La Bonne Auberge and Lawrence smiled across at her with all the charm of a watchful piranha.

She should have backed out when he'd arrived at her flat and his hands had lingered ever so slightly too long on her shoulders as he'd helped her into her coat. She should have told him to take her home when he'd kept patting her knee on the car journey here, but now she was trapped. Trapped with a man she didn't even like, until the meal was over and she could go home and shut the door on him.

'Can I say how very charming you look tonight, Nell?' Lawrence said, as the waiter offered him a menu and he took it without so much as a nod.

'I think you already have, Lawrence,' she replied. 'Many times, in fact.'

He leant towards her, probably one of the most fanciable men on the planet, provided you hadn't spent any time alone with him in an elevator, and his smile widened. 'A man can never pay a beautiful woman too many compliments.'

Oh, *please*, she thought. If you think that kind of flattery is going to get you anywhere, Lawrence, you're dumber than I thought.

'So, what's new in the world of Men's Surgical?' she said, and he wagged an admonishing finger at her.

'No shop talk tonight. Tonight is for us to get to know one another better.'

She didn't want to get to know him any better, she thought, but she managed a smile and tried not to notice that his eyes seemed incapable of remaining on her face but kept drifting downwards despite the high neckline of the deep green dress she'd deliberately chosen to wear this evening.

'The lady and I will have the watermelon, feta cheese and black olive salad,' Lawrence announced to the hovering waiter, 'followed by roast pheasant with panacetta and caramelised onions with a Madeira sauce.'

The lady would have liked to choose her own food, Nell thought, and it was on the tip of her tongue to say so but she bit back the comment quickly. *This is all in a good cause*, she told herself. *Just keep remembering, this is all in a good cause.*

'Why don't you tell me a little bit about yourself, Lawrence?' she said, and he did.

He told her all about the new car he'd just bought—'I insisted on the upholstery being real leather, of course'—and how he planned to spend only another couple of years at the Belfield— 'Glasgow is far too much of a backwater for a consultant like me'—and how he'd just been accepted as a member of one of the most prestigious London clubs—'It does help if you know the right people.'

It was boring, it was interminable, but she was just thinking that at least it meant she didn't have to do anything but nod and smile when Lawrence suddenly sat up straighter in his seat.

'Good grief, Jonah Washington's just arrived!' he exclaimed. 'And the girl with him…' His eyes widened appreciatively. 'I don't know who she is, but she's a real looker.'

She was. Tall, slender, with laughing eyes and a mass of brown curly hair that fell onto her shoulders in a way Nell knew she'd never get her own straight brown hair to fall, there was no mistaking who she was, and Nell wanted to crawl under the table and hide.

Why, oh, why had Jonah chosen tonight of all nights to bring Mary-Anne here? She'd *told* him she and Lawrence were having dinner at La Bonne Auberge, and for a moment she wondered if Jonah had deliberately selected this restaurant to annoy her, but that would have been petty, and he wasn't a petty man.

'I did hear he was dating somebody,' Lawrence continued, 'but I wonder how he managed to attract a girl like that?'

Nell didn't know, and at the moment couldn't have cared less. A brief nod in her direction had been the only indication Jonah had given that he'd seen her, but to sit here all evening knowing he was there was unbearable.

Eat fast, she told herself. Eat as fast as you can. But it was hard to eat quickly when the food suddenly tasted like cardboard, and even if she'd been able to wolf it down, Lawrence was clearly in no hurry.

He continued to discuss his favourite subject—himself—and Nell murmured 'I see' and 'How interesting' at what she hoped were appropriate moments and tried not to glance in Jonah's direction, but it was impossible.

That he liked Mary-Anne was plain. That she liked him was even more obvious, but it wasn't just the fact that they were so clearly enjoying each other's company that brought a lump to Nell's throat. It was the way they looked so right together. Right in a nice way. Right in a way couples who were completely at ease with one another always looked. There were no awkward pauses in their conversation, no artificial laughs. Jonah didn't even seem to feel the need to sit close to Mary-Anne to show the world she was his. He was simply content to be with her, to talk and to eat.

'Superb roast pheasant, isn't it?' Lawrence said, and Nell managed to nod.

Jonah would never have sent her an email saying their engagement was off. He would have flown back from New York and told her face to face. He would never have left her to brave the whispered comments and snide remarks at the Belfield alone. If he and Mary-Anne split up, and from their obvious closeness she didn't think it likely, he would be at Mary-Anne's side, fending off the comments, protecting her.

It wasn't Brian's fault, her heart whispered. *He would have come back and explained, but it was Candy who stopped him. It's her fault.*

But the words sounded feeble even to her own heart.

'You know, strange as it might seem, I prefer my date to spend her time looking at me, and listening to my conversation, rather than staring across the restaurant at another man.'

She looked round quickly to find Lawrence's eyes on her, and flushed.

'I *am* listening to you,' she began, all too conscious that the colour on cheeks was belying her words. 'I was just admiring the décor. The drapes are beautiful.'

'Nell, I may be a lot of things, but I'm not stupid,' Lawrence declared, his eyes cold, hard. 'This is all a scam, isn't it? You've clearly got the hots for Jonah Washington, he's not been paying you any attention at work, so this date is your way of trying to make him jealous.'

She stared at him in horror. 'No, oh, no, you couldn't possibly be more wrong.'

'I don't like being made a fool of Nell, and I don't like being conned, and this evening has "con" written all over it.'

Fury was plain in his face, but not just fury. She could see other emotions there, too. Disbelief, indignation and hurt. There was hurt in his eyes and, unbidden and unwanted, Jonah's words crept into her mind.

Everyone has feelings, Nell.

He'd been right, and she'd been wrong, so wrong. Lawrence might be a pompous, conceited jerk, but nobody deserved to be used, and that's what this whole evening had been about.

'Lawrence…'

He was getting to his feet. He was going to walk out on her, and though part of her was absolutely mortified, the other part, the considerably larger part, knew that though she deserved to be humiliated, this man didn't.

'Lawrence, I'm sorry, truly sorry,' she said quickly. 'I should never have accepted your invitation to dinner.'

'Then why did you?' he demanded, and she took a deep breath, knowing that what she was about to say had better be good because she owed this man. She owed him big time.

'I…I thought I was over Brian,' she said. 'That it was time for me to move on, to start dating again, but I'm not over him. Being dumped, it still hurts, and if I've been glancing over at Jonah and his girlfriend occasionally…' Big understatement there, Nell. 'It's because they remind me of how Brian and I used to be, of the times we shared.'

'I see.'

She hoped he did. She was also immensely relieved to see Jonah walking towards the toilets. Please, let him stay there, she prayed. Please, don't let him come back to witness my evening ending in a complete fiasco.

'I'll settle the bill,' Lawrence said, pulling his wallet out of his pocket, 'and then I'll drive you home.'

'There's no need,' she said. 'I'll get a taxi.'

'I'll drive you home,' he interrupted. 'Unlike some people, I have a sense of responsibility.'

She deserved that, she knew she did. She'd deserved considerably worse, she thought as Lawrence headed for the waiter who had served them and she pushed her scarcely touched plate away. Why in the world had she ever thought that going out with Lawrence was a good idea? It had been dumb, and ill-conceived, right from the start.

'Excuse me?'

She looked up to see Jonah's girlfriend standing in front of her, and wanted to die.

'I know this is going to sound awful,' the girl continued, 'but you've been staring across at me all evening—'

Oh, hell.

'—And I have such a terrible memory for faces that I wondered if I knew you.'

'No, you don't,' Nell said awkwardly. 'The man you're with, Jonah Washington—I work with him at the Belfield Infirmary.'

'Really?' Mary-Anne exclaimed. 'Jonah never talks to me about his work, so do tell. What's he like to work with?'

'Terrific,' Nell said simply, and to her surprise the girl's face fell.

'And there was me hoping you would dish the dirt so I could tease him mercilessly. Just kidding,' Mary-Anne continued with a smile as Nell stared at her. 'I love Jonah to bits.'

She loved him. Well, that was good, and if Nell's throat suddenly felt tight, she wasn't surprised. She'd had a lousy evening. She'd had a lousy fortnight since Brian's email, and the future wasn't looking any brighter.

'But I do like to wind him up occasionally. It stops him from becoming pompous. I'm Mary-Anne, by the way,' the girl added, holding out her hand, and Nell took it.

'I'm Nell. Nell Sutherland. Jonah has spoken a lot about you.'

'All bad, I expect.' Mary-Anne laughed. She looked over her shoulder to where Lawrence was talking to their waiter. 'Is there a problem with your meal?'

'Not a problem, no,' Nell said, feeling her cheeks heat up. 'The date—it's been a bit of a disaster so we're cutting it short.'

'Oh, I am sorry,' Mary-Anne said sympathetically. 'Look, would you like to join Jonah and me at our table?'

'Oh, no, thank you but no,' Nell said swiftly, scrabbling for her handbag. She'd rather be carried out with food poisoning than encroach on Jonah's date. 'Lawrence is going to drive me home.'

'We could give you a lift home,' Mary-Anne said. 'And it wouldn't be any imposition,' she continued as Nell opened her mouth to say just that. 'I'm staying with Jonah so it would only mean making a detour.'

So Mary-Anne wasn't just a girlfriend. She was a live-in girlfriend, and for no reason that Nell could fathom she suddenly wanted to burst into tears. PMT, she told herself. It's PMT, or maybe she was coming down with something, or maybe it was Lawrence. Yes, that was it. She was feeling guilty about Lawrence, and she deserved to.

'Nell, are you OK?'

There was concern on Mary-Anne's face, and Nell got to her feet fast.

'It was nice meeting you. I...I hope we meet again some time.' She turned to go, then paused. 'Would you tell Jonah that...' She bit her lip. 'Tell him he was right about everybody having feelings. He'll know what I mean,' she added as Jonah's girlfriend looked puzzled.

And with that she headed for the door, leaving Mary-Anne frowning after her.

Mary-Anne's frown deepened when Jonah came back to their table and she saw him glance immediately to where Nell had been sitting.

'She's gone,' she said. 'Your friend, Nell Sutherland, she's gone.'

He swivelled round fast in his seat. 'Gone where?'

'Home, I should imagine,' she said, but when she saw a muscle clench in his jaw she took pity on him. 'If it will make you feel any better, her date seems to have been a total disaster and this Lawrence person is simply driving her home.'

A look of relief appeared on his face, then his eyes shot to hers. 'How do you know her name's Nell Sutherland?'

'I introduced myself.'

He looked suddenly flustered. 'When you say introduced yourself, what exactly did you mean?'

'I told her my name was Mary-Anne.'

'And that's all you told her?' he pressed. 'You didn't tell her anything else?'

Her eyes narrowed. 'No, I didn't, and you look guilty, Jonah.'

'Rubbish,' he protested lightly, as dark colour began to creep up his neck. 'What do I have to be guilty about?'

She gave him a shrewd, assessing stare. 'You tell me.'

'Would you like some dessert?' he asked. 'The chef here does an amazing cappuccino slice with Tia Maria.'

Mary-Anne smiled. 'I'd love a slice, but that doesn't mean you're off the hook. If you won't tell me what this is all about, I'll find out myself. I always do, remember?'

Jonah laughed as he beckoned to their waiter. 'Not this time, Mary-Anne. Not this time.'

CHAPTER FIVE

'KATIE KELLY is scheduled for her standard eight-week premature eye test this morning,' Jonah said, taking a sip of his coffee before sitting down behind his desk. 'I've explained the procedure to her parents, but could you go over it with them again, Bea, make sure they understand?'

'Will do,' she replied.

'Donna Harrison had an excellent weekend in Transitional so unless either of you have any reservations or concerns, I'd like to discharge her today,' Jonah continued.

'I've no problems with that,' Bea said and, when Nell nodded her agreement, Jonah beamed.

'Terrific,' he said. 'Nell, do you want to phone Sheila, give her the good news?'

'I'll do it after this meeting,' she said, scribbling a reminder down in her notebook.

'Adam Thornton spent half an hour off his ventilator yesterday, which is good news, and Tommy Moffat actually put on a little more weight over the weekend, which is even better,' Jonah observed. He took another sip of his coffee and leant back in his seat. 'OK, that's my update for this morning. Do either of you have anything you'd like to raise?'

'Haematology,' Bea began, and as the ward sister launched into a list of complaints about the department, Nell stared down at her notebook and wished she were in some exotic location with Maddie and Gabriel, or back in bed under her duvet, or anywhere but here.

Her horrible weekend hadn't ended with Lawrence's tight-lipped 'Well, I can't say that was fun, Nell' after he'd driven her home on Saturday night. On Sunday afternoon she'd received another email from Brian.

If it's not too much trouble, he'd written, *could you parcel up and send on my two spare dress shirts? Candy's parents host a lot of charity events and the one dress shirt I brought with me is beginning to look rather the worse for wear.*

So am I, Brian, Nell thought as she'd read through the email, and I think I deserve a bit more consideration than your damned shirts. Where is the regret, the tiniest hint that you might occasionally think about me? All you're bothered about is your blasted shirts, whereas unless Lawrence keeps his big mouth shut, everybody at the Belfield is going to label me an idiot.

Jonah probably already thinks I am, she thought, sneaking a quick glance at him then looking away again fast in case he caught her eye, and it was all her own fault. She should never have told Mary-Anne the truth. She should have lied, said Lawrence had been paged by the hospital, but, no, she had to go and reveal all the sorry details, and Mary-Anne and Jonah had probably enjoyed a good laugh at her expense on Saturday night. Which hurt. Actually, it hurt even more than Brian's email had done.

'I'll have another talk with Haematology, Bea,' Jonah said, 'though I have to say I think they'll pull the old lack-of-staff excuse. I'll also, if Nell's in agreement, put forward your suggestion and see how they react.'

Bea had made a suggestion? Nell glanced from Bea to Jonah, then back again. What suggestion? Oh, damn and blast, that would teach her to not pay attention, but even the offer of a pair of brand-new Jimmy Choos wouldn't have made her admit she hadn't been listening.

'If…if you both think it's a good idea,' she began, 'then I'm all for it. Provided we thoroughly examine all the pros and cons, of course,' she added quickly, just in case she might have agreed to something she would never normally have given the time of day to.

'Would you like to examine all the pros and cons now?' Jonah said, and as his eyes met hers Nell saw a glint of amusement in them and wanted him dead.

He knew. He knew she hadn't been listening, and now he was trying to wind her up. Normally she would have laughed and come clean, but not today. Not after her miserable weekend, and certainly not with that ridiculously oversized photograph of Mary-Anne sitting on Jonah's desk, smirking at her.

'No, I wouldn't,' she said, closing her notebook with a snap. 'And if there's nothing else, I have work to do.'

Bea's mouth fell open in amazement but Nell didn't care. She knew she had just been quite unbelievably rude to Jonah but she wanted out of his consulting room-now-but as the ward sister headed for the door, and Nell made to follow her, Jonah got to his feet with a speed she wouldn't have expected from such a big man and barred her way.

'Can I have a word?' he said.

She didn't want to talk to him. She didn't want to hear him say 'I told you so' about Saturday night but telling your boss to get lost was not an option.

'It will have to be quick,' she replied, all super-efficient and professional on the outside as Bea threw her a concerned look before disappearing. 'I've a lot on my plate this morning.'

'I'll make this very quick,' he said, closing his consulting room door and leaning back against it as though he suspected she might make a run for it. 'What's wrong?'

'The same as usual,' she said. 'Too much paperwork, too few hours in which to do it.'

He shook his head. 'And that explains why you didn't hear a

word Bea said and snapping my head off? I don't think so. I think this has something to do with Saturday night.'

'Mind-reader now, are you?' she said, more icily than she'd intended, but she hadn't slept for days, her head was aching, and her heart and pride were hurting even more.

'Dammit, Nell, we're supposed to be friends—'

'You didn't tell me you had a girlfriend, or that you were a member of a band,' she exclaimed, all too aware she was sounding quite unbelievably childish but unable to stop herself. 'Friendship works both ways, Jonah.'

A dull tide of colour crept across his cheeks, and he had the grace to look uncomfortable.

'OK, I should have told you about Mary-Anne,' he conceded, 'and maybe I should have told you about the band. But Mary-Anne—' his eyes met hers '—told me your date with Lawrence wasn't a success, and that's why you left La Bonne Auberge early. He did just drive you home, didn't he?'

'No, he didn't,' she said. 'He sweet-talked me all the way back to my flat and then we made mad passionate love and it was so good we're doing it again this weekend.'

A muscle twitched in the side of his cheek. 'I see.'

'No, you don't,' she said wearily. 'My evening was a complete and utter fiasco, just like you said it would be, so why don't you just say it?'

'Say what?'

'I told you so.'

'You think I'm that smug?' He smiled, and she gave a short laugh.

'Yes.'

The smile on his lips hardened. 'Completely wrong and not very kind, Nell.'

'What did you expect?' she flared. 'That I should be grateful to you for being right while I was so spectacularly wrong? That

I shouldn't care that you and Mary-Anne probably had a good laugh about me on Saturday night?'

'I would never laugh at you, Nell,' he retorted, his face angry 'You might infuriate me, irritate the hell out of me at times, bu I would never laugh at you.'

'OK, so you didn't laugh,' she said, 'but don't expect me to be grateful that you were right about Lawrence. No norma person would be.'

'Nell—'

'Can I go now, please?' she interrupted.

He unfolded his arms and straightened up. 'Maybe we should start this conversation again. I'll pretend you didn't call me smug and you can pretend—'

'That we don't have any secrets from one another?' She shook her head. 'I think it's a bit late for that, Jonah, and I have work to do so could you move away from the door?'

For a second she didn't think he was going to then, with obvious reluctance, he stepped to one side and she swept past him and down the corridor to her own office and slammed the door behind her.

Never had she ever felt quite so out of sorts with him. For two years he'd been her friend, her confidant, her rock, yes, dammit her rock, and now he was being smug and patronising and....

No, he wasn't, she thought as she sat down at her desk and closed her eyes. It wasn't his fault he'd fallen in love with a beautiful girl while she was fast becoming the laughing stock of the Belfield. It wasn't his fault she felt lonely, unhappy and just plain *dumb*. He was a friend and you didn't own friends, shouldn't feel aggrieved if they kept parts of their lives separate from you. It was time she grew up. Time she stood on her own two feet and stopped relying on other people.

Maybe that was where she'd gone wrong with Brian. Maybe she had been too needy, too quick to agree to whatever he'd suggested, but she'd been so amazed when he'd fallen in love with her, had so wanted him to stay with her, that backing off from any argument had seemed a small price to pay.

'It'll be different when he comes back,' she told the empty room. '*I'll* be different when he comes back.'

But what if he doesn't come back? her heart whispered, and she shivered, though the unit was warm. She had to believe he would come back, because if he didn't... All she could see were years of loneliness stretching ahead of her.

And years on the unemployment line, she thought as she remembered Jonah's instructions about phoning Sheila Harrison.

'Brian will come back,' she said firmly as she reached for the phone. 'He has to.'

'I never thought this moment would come, Sister,' Sheila said later that morning as she adjusted the shawl round her small daughter and held her closer. 'I know Donna hasn't been in the unit for anywhere near as long as some of the other babies, but to be finally able to take her home...

'She's a terrible worrier, my wife,' Sheila's husband said, but Nell could see the relief in his eyes.

She could also see that the novelty of being in the unit had worn off for the couple's other two children and they were becoming thoroughly bored.

'Don't forget to phone us if you're worried about anything,' she said, gently steering the family towards the unit door. 'Not that I think you will be,' she added quickly, in case she was putting ideas into Sheila's head. 'Donna is a beautiful, healthy baby.'

'I wish I could have thanked Dr Jonah personally,' Sheila said. 'Without him...'

She trailed off, and Nell gave her a hug.

'He was hoping to see you, too,' she said, 'but I'm afraid the consultant from Ophthalmology is with him at the moment.'

He'd been with him for the past hour, Nell thought, glancing surreptitiously at her watch, which meant either Mr Brentwood liked extremely long coffee-breaks or something was wrong with Katie Kelly's eyes and she was keeping her fingers crossed that the ophthalmologist was a caffeine addict.

'Thanks for everything, Sister,' Sheila continued, 'and you take care of yourself, you hear? You've been looking really tired lately.'

In other words, she looked terrible, Nell thought as she waved the family goodbye, and she knew she did. Lack of sleep didn't suit her, neither did living on her own. With nobody to cook for she'd been slipping badly from her diet, and it showed.

'Are you lunching in the canteen today?' Fiona asked, coming out of her office just as Nell passed by. 'I understand the special is lasagne.'

For a second Nell's mouth watered, then she remembered her waistline.

'I think I might just pick up a sandwich and bring it back to my office,' she said, and Fiona beamed.

'Could you bring me one, too? Cheese and salad for preference, but if they're all out of those I'll settle for a chicken and mayo. I've still got to lose four more kilos before I'm back to the weight I was before I had George.'

I wasn't the weight you are now when I was ten years old, Nell thought as she headed for the elevator, then shook her head.

Self-pity, her mind whispered, and self-pity is destructive, corrosive. Why should Brian want to come back to a girl who's become a wimp? He wants you to be the way you were when he first met you. Outgoing, positive, assertive, so pull yourself together.

And, for God's sake, smile, she told herself when the elevator reached the ground floor and she saw Liz walking towards her.

'The very person I was hoping to see,' the obs and gynae sister announced, rummaging through her shoulder-bag and producing a sheet of paper. 'Could you give this to Jonah for me? It's his disclaimer form, removing any responsibility from the hospital for any injuries he might sustain in the talent contest on Wednesday night.

'Injuries?' Nell repeated. 'But I thought he and his band were just singing a few songs?'

Liz pulled a face. 'They are, but Admin's stressing in case somebody falls off the stage in the function suite and then sues the Belfield for damages. Are you coming to the show?'

'Wouldn't miss it.'

'I've only seen Jonah and his friends rehearse once because of his shifts,' Liz continued, 'but they're really good. In fact, I wouldn't be at all surprised if they won.'

Neither would Nell when she considered the competition Jonah was up against.

'Did you know his group—they're called The Medics, by the way…'

Oh, barf, Nell thought.

'They're a tribute band?'

A tribute band? Oh, dear lord, please don't let it be *Queen*, Nell thought in dismay. Her uncle always did his impersonation of Freddie Mercury at family weddings and it was absolutely mortifying.

'What band are they a tribute to?' she said with foreboding, and Liz smiled.

'My all-time favourite, Elvis.'

Nell opened her mouth, then closed it again

How in the world could a four-man band pay tribute to Elvis Presley? Elvis had been a solo singer, not part of a group, and suddenly she had a horrible vision of Jonah and his three friends turning up on Wednesday night wearing identical white Lycra jumpsuits.

'Liz, about Jonah's band—' she began, but Liz was already stepping into the elevator.

'I've got to go, Nell,' she said. 'Andrew Portman's stressing about his white pigeons. Apparently they're an integral part of his act, but one's gone off its food.'

'But, Liz—'

She was too late. The elevator doors had already shut and she was left talking to thin air.

What the hell was she going to do? she wondered as she walked down to the canteen and bought a sandwich for herself and one for Fiona. She could hardly tell Jonah to pull out of the contest. She wasn't his mother, he wasn't a child, but a tribute band to Elvis Presley? It was just so not Jonah, but, then, a lot of the things he'd been doing over the part fortnight hadn't been him either. Maybe he was experiencing some sort of mid-life crisis. Maybe he was going to start turning up for work wearing skin-tight trousers and sporting an earring in his ear.

A splutter of laughter sprang to her lips, a splutter that became a guffaw as she left the canteen. It would be worth it just to see Lawrence Summers's face.

Only not today, she thought, skidding to a halt when she saw the man himself standing by the elevators. And he wasn't alone. Mary-Anne was with him, and swiftly Nell ducked into the hospital florist's.

This is ridiculous, she told herself as she hovered beside the buckets of flowers and helium balloons with congratulatory messages written on them. What did it matter if Lawrence and Mary-Anne saw her?

It mattered because Lawrence would undoubtedly cut her dead after Saturday night. It mattered because Mary-Anne might ask him to tell her more about their date, and Jonah's girlfriend already knew too much.

Yes, but you can't hide in here for ever, her mind argued. The florist was already beginning to give her odd looks, and maybe Lawrence and Mary-Anne had gone.

They hadn't.

Even a three-year-old would have known that Mary-Anne was flirting quite shamelessly with Lawrence and, as Nell stared in open-mouthed horror at her, Jonah's girlfriend suddenly looked up and saw her. And she smiled. She had the unmitigated gall to smile, and Nell's horror turned to anger. A white-hot anger that had her stepping forward, fully intending to give the pair of them a piece of her mind, only for her to realise she couldn't, because what could she say?

Mary-Anne, you're standing way too close to Lawrence, and, Lawrence, stop drooling?

Standing too close to somebody and drooling were hardly capital crimes, and if she shrieked, *Mary-Anne, you're a cheating bitch*, and *Lawrence, you're lower than a snake's waistcoat button*, she'd look a fool, and she'd already looked like a fool in their company.

She would tell Jonah, but no sooner had the thought popped into her head than she knew she wouldn't. What man would want to know that the woman he loved was flirting with another man?

All she could do was to pretend she hadn't seen them. Take the stairs instead of the elevator, and pretend she hadn't seen them.

'You've been gone a while,' Fiona said when Nell arrived in her office. 'Was there a queue?'

'Yes,' Nell muttered. 'They didn't have cheese and salad so I got you chicken and mayo.'

'Great.' Fiona took the sandwich Nell was holding out to her, then frowned. 'You all right?'

'A bit puffed.' Nell lied. 'I took the stairs instead of the elevator.'

'Maybe I should try that,' Fiona said, then chuckled. 'And then again, perhaps not. Jonah left a message to say he'd like to see you a.s.a.p.'

Jonah wanted to see her? A few minutes ago her main worry had been him appearing in Wednesday's talent contest looking like Elvis in his Las Vegas days, but now she was going to have to face him knowing what she knew, and that was worse. Much worse.

Deliberately she dawdled over her lunch-break, then even more deliberately she hovered around Special Care, though it quickly became apparent that she wasn't needed.

'No problems with the syringe, Viv?' she asked, as she

watched the girl inject a syringe full of her own breast milk into her son's feeding tube.

'It was fiddly to start with, but I'm getting the hang of it now,' Viv replied. 'And I like doing it. Makes me feel useful.'

'If Callum continues to progress the way he's doing, you'll soon be able to feed him with a bottle,' Nell said.

'Roll on that day.' Viv laughed, and Nell laughed with her, but she knew she was simply postponing the inevitable.

Forget that you saw Mary-Anne with Lawrence, Nell told herself as she left the unit and walked slowly down the corridor towards Jonah's consulting room. If you tell him what you saw, you'll just stir up a heap of trouble so forget about it. It sounded convincing, it sounded sensible, so why did she feel so guilty?

Jonah didn't look any happier than she felt when she went into his consulting room.

'You wanted to see me?' she said, and he nodded.

'Katie Kelly.'

'Katie?' she repeated, momentarily thrown, and then she remembered that the ophthalmologist had stayed with Jonah for a very long time after he'd examined the little girl's eyes. 'What did Mr Brentwood say?'

'Retinopathy of prematurity. A classic case, according to Brentwood,' Jonah declared, not bothering to hide his sarcasm, 'except that Katie isn't a case, she's a little girl.'

'Did he give you any idea of how bad it is?' she asked as she sat down, and Jonah shook his head.

'He wants to do further tests this afternoon and tomorrow, and hopes to have the results back by Thursday.' He bit his lip. 'She was doing so well, Nell. Spectacularly well for a ten and a half week preemie, and now this.'

She could understand his frustration. They had no way of knowing which babies would develop retinopathy of prematurity. No way of proving that a baby even had ROP until they were given an eye test eight weeks before what would have been their due date, and by then the damage to their sight had been done.

'Would laser surgery help her sight?' she said, and Jonah sighed.

'If it's as bad as Brentwood fears, I doubt it.'

He was right and, ironically, it was preemies' exposure to the oxygen they needed to keep them alive that could lead to the sudden growth of abnormal blood vessels in their eyes. Once those blood vessels began to multiply they could cause bleeding and, in a worst-case scenario, intensive scarring that led to the retina actually peeling away from the back of the eye.

'What are you going to tell her parents?' she asked, and he leant back in his seat.

'Nothing until Brentwood gives me a definite prognosis.'

'But surely they have a right to know what the possibilities might be?' she protested, and saw a flash of anger darken Jonah's brown eyes.

'You think they'll want to know Katie might be completely blind? "Sufficient unto the day," as my old granny used to say, and on this occasion I think she's right.'

'But—'

'My decision, Nell,' he said firmly, and though she knew it was, she could not help but think his decision was wrong.

At the very least she would have warned Katie's parents that the prognosis might not be good, but she sensed Jonah was in denial, not least because he had always been so positive about Katie.

'It's not your fault, Jonah,' she said gently. 'Katie's eyes, there's nothing you could have done to prevent it happening.'

'I know, but knowing that doesn't make it any easier for me to accept,' he said, then slammed his fist down on the desk with such force that she jumped. 'What we need is to be able to prevent ROP from developing at all.'

'It will happen,' she said, reaching out to cover his hand with her own. 'Look at the difference laser surgery has already made to minor cases, and don't some scientists believe there's a protein called HIF-2a which might also contribute to the development of retinopathy of prematurity, and they think that if they can figure out a way of shutting it down we might be able to prevent blindness from ever occurring?'

'Yes, but none of this will help Katie right now, will it?' Jonah said.

'No, but at least it means there's hope for other babies, in the future,' she said.

For a moment his hand remained rigid beneath hers, then he sighed.

'And we have to think that way, don't we?' he said. 'We have to be optimists or we wouldn't be able to function.'

And she wished he'd get rid of that damn photograph, Nell thought, trying not to let her eyes drift to Mary-Anne's picture, but it was so big it was virtually impossible.

'She's terrific, isn't she?' Jonah said, seeing the direction of her gaze. 'So full of fun and life.'

And she spreads it about, Nell thought, but no way was she going to tell him that.

'I…I'm glad you've found somebody you like,' she said instead.

'Are you?'

His voice sounded oddly husky, and she dragged her gaze away from Mary-Anne's photograph, fully prepared to lie and give the girl a glowing report, only to find that she couldn't say anything at all when her eyes met his because her heart suddenly performed a most extraordinary back flip against her rib cage.

Which was weird. It was more than weird because they must have had hundreds of conversations over the past two years and her heart had always stayed resolutely stationary in her chest.

'Nell?'

'I… Of—of course I'm pleased,' she stammered. 'You're my friend, and I want you to be happy.'

'Do you?'

His voice sounded even huskier, and was it her imagination or had his consulting room suddenly become very warm? It felt warm. So did she. In fact, she felt hot. Very hot.

Maybe she was coming down with something. Half the Belfield staff were coughing and wheezing, but she didn't feel as though she was getting a cold. She felt strange. Tingling, expectant and breathless. Definitely breathless.

'Jonah,' she began, then had to stop because he'd turned his fingers round under hers so that he was holding her hand and her heart had performed another weird back flip.

Palpitations. She was developing palpitations. She'd certainly endured enough stress in the past three weeks, with her new job, then Brian dumping her and her awful date with Lawrence, but surely if she was suffering from palpitations she would have had some prior warning?

'Yes, Nell?'

Yes, what? she wondered. For the life of her she couldn't remember what they'd been talking about. All she was aware of was the gentle touch of his fingers around hers, and his eyes—had they always been that dark liquid brown colour? They must have been and yet she'd never noticed. She was noticing now. She was noticing big time, and she tried to suck in some air but that didn't help because she saw something flare in his eyes that sent her heart rate into overdrive.

The last time she'd felt so strange had been when she'd fallen in love with Brian, but she wasn't falling in love with Jonah. Good grief, she'd known him for two years, and you didn't wait two years to fall in love with a man. It was something that happened instantly. You saw a man then, wham, you knew you were in love. It wasn't something that crept up on you.

'You were talking about Mary-Anne,' Jonah prompted softly, 'and whether she was the right woman for me.'

You have such lovely hair, Jonah. Soft, silky.

He did, too, she thought as she stared back at him, completely unable to look away, and the way his white coat was tightening across his chest as he leant towards her was almost…sexy.

No, it wasn't sexy. Where in the world had that idea come from? This was Jonah, her best friend, her mate. Jonah wasn't sexy, Brian was. And yet she was hyperventilating, she knew she was, until her eyes fell on Mary-Anne's photograph again and suddenly she didn't feel like hyperventilating at all.

'Jonah, Mary-Anne's a very pretty girl, but are you absolutely certain she's the right girl for you?'

'You think there might be someone else?'

Me.

No, forget me, ignore me. I don't know why I thought me. I'm in love with Brian, and you're in love with Mary-Anne, except she's a bitch and she's going to hurt you badly.

'Nell?'

Her thudding heart slowed and a wave of guilt crept over her. How would she have felt if somebody had known about Brian and Candy and not told her? Humiliated. Completely and utterly humiliated. She had to tell Jonah. Somehow she had to tell him.

'Jonah.'

Say it, Nell, say it.

'Mary-Anne… She's a lovely girl, but you and I both know there's a certain kind of woman who… Well, who what they want most in life is status, position.'

He smiled. 'I've always thought glass ceilings were wrong, that women should be able to rise to the top of their professions and not be held back because of their sex.'

Oh, hell, that wasn't what she'd meant at all.

'I agree,' she said, nodding manically, 'but when I said status, position, I didn't mean women earning that for themselves. I meant, I meant that there are women, not all women, but some women who, um, when they see a man like you, a nice man, a kind man, a man who is a specialist registrar and who will one day become a consultant, they see security, status, a future, and

Mary-Anne, well, I'm wondering if she….if she's not the sort…the kind of woman who…'

Her voice trailed away into silence. All the warmth in his eyes had gradually disappeared as she'd been speaking and in its place was anger. An anger so blazing that she involuntarily sat further back in her seat.

'I'm sorry, I'm not explaining this very well,' she began, but he didn't let her finish.

'I think you're explaining it perfectly,' he interrupted, releasing her hand as though it stung. 'You're saying I'm so bloody boring that the only reason Mary-Anne, or any other woman, might be interested in me is because I might become a consultant one day. Well, thanks, Nell, thanks for nothing.'

'Jonah—'

'This conversation is over,' he said, his face a cold, white mask of fury. 'Close the door on your way out.'

'But, Jonah—'

'Are you deaf as well as arrogant?' he roared, and Nell took one look at his face and fled.

She didn't see him bang his fist down on the desk again, sending the photograph of Mary-Anne toppling over with a bang. Neither did she see him kick the waste-paper basket that some fool had left near his desk, sending it ricocheting across his consulting room so that it landed with a resounding thud against the opposite wall. Nor did she see him get grimly to his feet to make one last tour of the unit before he went home, determined to wipe the dust of the Belfield, and everybody in it, off his feet.

'Will pasta for dinner be OK tonight?' Mary-Anne called from the kitchen as Jonah let himself into his flat. 'Or, then again, perhaps not,' she added as she came out into the hallway and saw his face. 'Perhaps you'd prefer me to make up a very large bowl of strychnine for whoever's got right up your nose.'

'Very amusing,' Jonah said tightly. 'Pasta's fine.'

'Rough day?' she said, watching him throw his car keys down on the hall table.

'You could say that.'

'I was there today. At the Belfield,' Mary-Anne said, following him into the sitting room. 'I came to see you but bumped into Lawrence Summers.'

'That must have been fun for you,' he said, sitting down on the sofa and letting his head fall back against it, and Mary-Anne smiled.

'Lawrence may be a creep, but he's also a very interesting creep. He told me all about Nell's fiancé dumping her. He also thinks Nell is stuck on you but you don't realise it.'

'Mary-Anne…'

'I think he's wrong,' she said, ignoring the warning in Jonah's voice. 'I think you're stuck on her and she doesn't realise it.'

'None of this is any of your business, Mary-Anne,' he said firmly, but she sat down on the sofa beside him, her face determined.

'I think it's very much my business when you've obviously told Nell I'm your girlfriend, and what I want to know is why any sane man would pretend that his sister was his girlfriend.'

'It's complicated,' he said awkwardly, and Mary-Anne folded her arms across her chest.

'I've got all night.'

Jonah loosened his tie and dropped it over the arm of the sofa, looking wearier than Mary-Anne had ever seen him.

'I pretended you were my girlfriend because I had the crazy idea that it would make Nell realise I'm a man. She never has, you see. For the two years I've known her she's only ever seen me as a friend.'

'But wouldn't it have been easier simply to come right out and tell her how you feel?' Mary-Anne protested. 'Wouldn't that have shown her you're a man?'

'She was engaged, sis.'

'Not when you first met her, she wasn't,' his sister replied, then her eyes narrowed. 'It's Rowan, isn't it? You've got yourself into this mess with Nell because of Rowan. Oh, Jonah, I know she hurt you, messed you around, but I'd bet the Rolex watch you gave me last Christmas that Nell's not like that.'

'It doesn't matter any more,' he interrupted grimly. 'It's over, finished. Nell told me this afternoon that the only woman who would ever be interested in me would be a woman looking to further her own social status.'

'I can't believe she said that,' Mary-Anne retorted. 'You must have misunderstood.'

'Sis, I was there,' he retorted. 'We were talking about you, and whether you were the right girl for me, and…' He came to a halt as his sister suddenly began to laugh. 'You think this is funny?'

'You bet I think it's funny because I know why Nell said what she did. She saw me getting up close and personal with Lawrence at lunchtime. Look, I was trying to get some information out of him, OK?' she added as her brother groaned. 'You wouldn't tell me anything, and I figured Lawrence might, and he did, and now Nell clearly thinks I'm cheating on you.'

'Mary-Anne, I could wring your neck,' he said, and his sister's jaw dropped.

'You could wring my neck? Jonah, don't you realise what a dangerous game you're playing? At some point you're going to have to tell Nell the truth and she's going to think you've set her up, made a fool of her. If you did that to me, you'd be toast.'

'That's because you're my sister,' he replied, and Mary-Anne shook her head.

'That's because I'm a woman, Jonah. Believe me, no woman likes to look stupid.'

She was wrong, Jonah thought as he stared at his sister's exasperated face. Nell would understand, he knew she would, and he couldn't stop now, not when his plan looked as though it might be working. This afternoon, before his talk with Nell had gone right down the tube, he'd been sure he'd seen something in Nell's eyes, an awareness of him that hadn't been there before, so no way was he going to tell her the truth. Not yet, at any rate.

'I know what I'm doing, Mary-Anne.'

'Jonah—'

'Back off, sis,' he said, and Mary-Anne said something utterly unrepeatable before she headed off back to the kitchen to torture the pasta.

CHAPTER SIX

'So you don't think Dr Jonah will give the go-ahead to try bottle-feeding Callum today?' Viv Nicolson said as she accompanied Nell into Special Care.

'I have to say I think it's unlikely,' Nell replied. 'Though Callum is doing very well, his muscle tone isn't as good as a full-term baby's yet and that can lead to reflux—a baby spitting back his feed—and we don't want him losing weight rather than putting it on.'

'I know.' Viv sighed. 'It's just I'd feel one step closer to eventually taking him home if I could bottle-feed him.'

'I'm sure it won't be much longer,' Nell said reassuringly. 'Callum's getting stronger every day.'

'That's what Dr Jonah said.' Viv looked around the unit and shivered. 'But I hate this place, Sister. No offence meant to you or the rest of the staff, you're all wonderful, but if I could just take Callum home I'd feel I was actually a proper mum.'

'You're already a proper mum, Viv,' Nell reassured her. 'You're feeding Callum with the syringe, bathing him, cuddling him, while Sister Bea, Dr Jonah and myself, are—'

'Just the medics,' Viv finished for her with a forced smile. 'That's what Dr Jonah keeps telling me, too. I hope he's in a better mood today—Dr Jonah, I mean. On Monday afternoon...' The girl shook her head '...somebody must have rubbed him up the wrong way big time because he was really snippy and that's not like him.'

Tell me about it, Nell thought. Being all but thrown out of Jonah's consulting room on Monday afternoon hadn't been pleasant. Not that she blamed him. She would have blown a fuse too, if somebody had implied Brian was only interested in her as a meal ticket, but she'd deliberately been keeping out of Jonah's way for the last two days to give him time to calm down.

Oh, come clean, Nell, a small voice whispered in her head. *That's not why you've been avoiding him.* You've been avoiding him because you're still freaked out by the weird feelings you experienced in his consulting room just before you tried to tell him about Mary-Anne.

Stress, she told the little voice firmly. The palpitations, the hot flushes had been due to nothing more than stress. No wonder she was stressed. She was under a lot of pressure at work, and Brian dumping her still hurts.

And you suddenly thinking Jonah looked sexy? the voice demanded. *Was that because of stress, too?*

That was just a…a temporary aberration, she told the annoying voice, a moment of madness. I'm missing Brian, the great sex we had together, and because Jonah's always been so supportive I simply mistook my feelings for something other than what they were.

Oh, really? the little voice mocked, and unconsciously she let out a huff of impatience.

'You don't think Dr Jonah's normally pretty laid back?' Viv said curiously, and Nell's cheeks prickled with heat.

She really had to stop her mind wandering like this. It had never happened to her before, not even when Brian had first told her he loved her. She might have gone around smiling like an idiot at everyone for no particular reason, but she'd always managed to keep her mind on her job, whereas just lately she seemed to be constantly drifting off into a fantasy land.

'Of course he is,' she said quickly, and Viv smiled.

But not at her, Nell realised with a sinking heart, seeing the direction of Viv's gaze.

Jonah. She'd bet a pound to a penny that Jonah had just come into Special Care, and a swift glance over her shoulder confirmed she was right.

Terrific. That was all she needed on a dreary Wednesday morning. Jonah cutting her dead.

Except he didn't. To her amazement he headed straight towards her with a beaming smile, as though Monday had never happened.

'Beautiful day, isn't it?' he said.

Viv glanced out of the unit window and shook her head.

'Doctor, it's absolutely foul out there,' she protested, and Jonah's smile widened.

'When you're happy inside, Viv, it's always a beautiful day,' he said, and Nell's heart sank even further.

If he was happy then he either hadn't confronted Mary-Anne with what she'd said or Mary-Anne, cunning bitch that she was, had soft-soaped him. Well, she'd done her best, Nell decided as she watched Jonah scan Callum's chart. No friend could do more, and from now on she was butting out of his private life.

'I was hoping I might be able to start bottle-feeding Callum today,' Viv said, her face hopeful, expectant.

'Not today, Viv,' Jonah replied. 'We'll try him on bottle feeds soon, but not today.'

'How soon is soon?' Viv demanded, and Jonah's brown eyes twinkled.

'Soon, Viv, and that's as much of a forecast as I'm prepared to give you. And now, if you'll excuse me,' he continued, 'I need to speak to Sister Nell.'

Without waiting for Viv to reply, he steered Nell towards the door.

'She wasn't pressurising you, Jonah,' Nell said as soon as

they were safely out in the corridor. 'She just so wants to take Callum home.'

'I know,' he said, 'but I need to ask you something. Ian Moffat, Tommy's father. When was the last time you saw him in Intensive?'

Nell frowned for a moment, then shook her head. 'A week, maybe ten days ago? I'm sorry, I can't be more specific.'

'Neither can Bea,' Jonah said grimly, 'which confirms what I've been suspecting. Helen's visiting her son, but Ian isn't.'

'Maybe he comes in when neither Bea nor I are here?' Nell suggested. 'Some fathers visit late at night.'

'And Ian isn't one of them,' Jonah interrupted. 'I've checked with the night staff and they can't remember when they last saw him either. It looks like I'll have to telephone him, read him the Riot Act about the importance of visiting. In fact, I think I'll go one step further. Insist he comes in to see me so we can talk face to face.'

'Do you think that's wise?' Nell said hesitantly. 'Some fathers get really spooked by NICU, and Ian's always struck me as a pretty mild-mannered sort of man. It might not be the best idea to pressurise him.'

'Nell, the man's Tommy's father,' Jonah protested. 'I might loathe the dentist, but if any kid of mine needed to go to one I sure as hell would be there with him.'

He would, too, Nell thought, and woe betide any dentist who accidentally inflicted pain on his child, but that didn't mean she agreed with him about Ian Moffat. Confronting the man with his failure to visit his son wouldn't have been her first course of action, but after Jonah's explosion on Monday the last thing she wanted was to provoke another row.

What she wanted was for them to return to their old, comfortable relationship, and as he had made the first step she was more than willing to meet him halfway.

'You must be getting nervous about the talent contest tonight,' she said, as he began to walk towards Intensive Care and she followed him.

'Nah. It's just another gig as far as I'm concerned.'

'But aren't you worried people might heckle you, or worse?' she said, and he smiled.

'I've performed at wedding receptions that resembled war zones so I don't think a little heckling is going to bother me.'

Want to bet? she thought. At least when he left wedding receptions he never had to see the guests again, but the audience tonight would consist of his colleagues and if his act was awful he'd never live it down.

Maybe she could fake a heart attack. Even if Jonah had given her an ear-blasting on Monday he was still her friend, so if people started heckling him maybe she could slump to the floor. Jonah would be sure to accompany her to A and E, and when they found nothing wrong she could smile sweetly and say, sorry, it must have been indigestion, and they'd never be able to prove otherwise.

'Will you be there tonight?' Jonah asked, almost as though he'd read her mind, and she nodded as he pushed open the door to Intensive Care, then stood aside to allow her to go ahead of him

'We'll all be there—Bea, Fiona and me.'

'Mary-Anne's coming, too.'

Oh, terrific. That was all she needed and, with her current run of luck the cheating bitch would probably end up sitting next to her.

'I owe you an apology for Monday, don't I?' Jonah continued, clearly misinterpreting her silence. 'I overreacted, yelled at you when I shouldn't have.'

'There's no need to apologise,' she muttered. 'I shouldn't have said what I did.'

Not that I didn't mean it, but I should have known better than to have tried to interfere.

'Mary-Anne…' Jonah cleared his throat, and to Nell's surprise he looked more uncomfortable than she could ever remember seeing him. 'She told me you saw her with Lawrence on Monday and that you, well, you might have misinterpreted her friendliness towards him.'

Like hell she had misinterpreted anything, but nothing on earth would have induced her to say so.

'Can't we just forget about Monday?' she said instead, and for a second he stared at her, his face a strange mixture of relief and uncertainty, then he laughed.

A laugh that sounded oddly contrived, and nothing at all like Jonah's normal laugh.

'That's what I told Mary-Anne,' he declared. 'She's a very friendly person, you see, always hugging everybody. But it's just her way.'

Yeah, right, she thought, and if you believe that then you'll believe anything.

'Adam was off his ventilator for forty minutes yesterday, and for almost fifty minutes this morning,' she said, deliberately changing the conversation.

'Terrific,' Jonah replied, clearly deciding, like her, that it was better to drop the subject of Mary-Anne. 'The sooner we can transfer him back to Special, the better. We're at full capacity in Intensive, and if Maternity suddenly needs an incubator we're sunk.'

Nell nodded. There had been a couple of occasions in the past when they'd had to tell a mother who had just given birth that although she would be remaining at the Belfield, her baby would have to be transferred to Edinburgh or Newcastle, and it had been heartbreaking.

'Let's reduce the ratio of oxygen in his ventilator, and see how he gets on,' Jonah continued. 'But if he shows any sign of distress, let me know immediately.'

'Did Bea tell you Tommy's gained another couple of grams since the weekend?' Nell said. 'And he was off his ventilator for fifteen minutes this morning. And before you ask,' she continued, seeing Jonah open his mouth, 'there have been no adverse effects.'

Jonah grinned as he unfurled his stethoscope and walked over to Tommy's incubator. 'Getting predictable, am I?'

'Nope,' Nell replied, 'but I know how worried you've been about his slow growth rate.'

'He may be small but he's certainly got plenty of attitude,' Jonah observed as he began examining Tommy and the little boy waved his small fists at him. 'Hey, relax, tiger. I'm not going to hurt you.'

Jonah wouldn't either, Nell thought as she watched him. He might be a big man, but she'd seen him insert the tiniest catheter into a baby weighing little more than a kilo with as much ease as he would tie his own shoelaces. She'd also seen him eject a drunken father on one memorable occasion, sending the man spinning out into the corridor as though he had been nothing more than an annoying fly.

'What's funny?'

She looked up to find Jonah's eyes on her and chuckled.

'I was just remembering Matt Spencer.'

Jonah frowned. 'Matt who?'

'Father of Elliot, two-and-a-half-kilo preemie, born two months premature last June,' she said. 'Matt turned up blind drunk in the unit one day and you threw him out.'

'I remember.' Jonah nodded. 'Admin warned me I was on my own if he decided to sue. What on earth made you think of him?'

Nell shrugged. 'I don't know,' she said, but she did.

Like Matt Spencer, she knew from personal experience how strong Jonah's hands were. They'd been strong enough not just to lift her up off the floor but also to carry her through to her bedroom on the awful night of Wendy's leaving bash. He deserved a medal, she thought ruefully, but as she continued to watch Jonah, she suddenly remembered something else. Something she'd forgotten about until now.

He'd touched her cheek that night just before she'd passed out. It had hardly been a touch at all, just the gentlest brushing of his fingers against her skin, but it had been enough to send a whirlwind of sensations coursing through her. Enough to make her shiver with pleasure and long for those fingers to touch her elsewhere. On her breasts, her thighs, her…

And she was doing it again, she realised with horror. Fantasising. Of course his touch hadn't done any of those things. It couldn't have. She'd been drunk, out of her head, so how could she possibly remember one touch?

But she did.

'Nell?'

Jonah's eyes were on her again, and for a fraction of a second their eyes locked then she looked quickly away, the colour of her cheeks darkening to crimson.

Therapy. She needed therapy, and she needed it fast. This was Jonah, for heaven's sake. Big, dependable, ordinary Jonah, and the fantasies she kept having about him, the weird thoughts they were crazy, stupid.

She had been desperately unhappy that night, she told herself as she stared fixedly down at Tommy, so if she'd had any thoughts, feelings, it had probably been because she'd been thinking of Brian, confusing Jonah with Brian.

'Nell.'

Oh, criminy, but his voice sounded exactly as it had in his consulting room on Monday, all deep and husky, and she knew if she looked up she was going to make a complete and utter fool of herself and their friendship would be over.

'Would you like me to speak to Helen about her husband not visiting Tommy?' she said, her eyes darting from the pulse oximeter taped to Tommy's little foot to the IV tube in his arm to the little hat on his head. 'We get on very well, and she might be more forthcoming in a woman-to-woman conversation.'

'Nell, look at me.'

Not even for the promise of the latest Gucci handbag, she thought, or at least not right now. Give her half an hour to pull herself together, ten minutes, and then she'd be able to, but not right now.

'It would be no trouble—speaking to Helen, I mean,' she babbled, fiddling awkwardly with the catheter in Tommy's umbilical stump. 'I could perhaps suggest that Ian speaks to our chaplain.'

'Nell, will you, *please*, look at me?'

Oh, double criminy. *Somebody—anybody—get me out of here*, she thought desperately, and, as though in answer to her prayer, the unit door opened and Bea appeared.

'Sorry to interrupt,' the ward sister exclaimed, 'but Fiona would like a word with you, Nell, if you've got a minute.'

If? Nell was out the unit door and running. With luck, whatever Fiona wanted would take ages to sort out, and then she was absolutely and definitely going to sign herself up for some therapy. With an elderly psychiatrist with a calm voice and a large leather chaise longue, who would pat her on the hand, tell her he'd dealt with hundreds of cases like hers and, no, she wasn't turning into a complete flake, but was totally normal.

'So, to recap,' Fiona said. 'In future you must complete all referrals from Maternity in triplicate, GP notes are not to be sent directly by you to the GP but have to go to Admin first, and pharmaceutical forms are always to be completed in black and not blue ink and on paper as well as on your computer.'

'Right,' Nell said, and the secretary looked at her a little uncertainly.

'Look, I'm only repeating what Admin said. It's not my fault if these instructions are dumb.'

'Pay no attention to me.' Nell sighed as she helped herself to a biscuit from the box on the secretary's desk. 'I'm not having a good day.'

'Would you like another coffee?' Fiona suggested. 'I always find the world looks a lot brighter after a coffee. Of course, it looks even brighter after a couple of glasses of wine,' she added with a grin, 'but I think Admin would cut up rough if we went around drunk all the time.'

Nell didn't know about Admin but she knew she was never going to drink again. From now on she was going to remain strictly teetotal. Life was safer that way.

'Bea, have you time for a quick coffee?' Fiona called, seeing the ward sister pass her office door.

'Having just had my ear bent for the last twenty minutes by Liz Fenton, I need the whole pot,' Bea replied, and Nell's eyebrows rose.

'Is there a problem with the talent contest tonight?'

Bea shook her head. 'Liz is under pressure because Admin are insisting it should be a seats-only affair for safety reasons, and apparently she's sold more tickets than the function suite has seats.'

'I'm not surprised, ' Fiona said, handing Nell and Bea their coffees. 'Nobody wants to miss out on the chance of seeing their colleagues make complete idiots of themselves.'

'Do we know who's judging tonight?' Nell asked, taking a bite of her biscuit.

'Olivia Hardcastle from A and E, Cynthia Braithwaite from Pharmacy and Lawrence Summers from Surgical. Hey, are you OK?' Fiona said as Nell coughed and spluttered breathlessly.

'Crumb,' Nell gasped. 'Down the wrong way. No need to panic.'

Except Lawrence being selected as one of the judges was the last thing she wanted. It was bad enough that he was still being less than friendly whenever they met, but since her disastrous date with him he had seemed to take great delight in making snide comments about Jonah, almost as though he somehow held him personally responsible for the debacle.

'I have to say I'm really looking forward to the contest,' Bea declared. 'Especially to seeing Jonah perform.'

Fiona's eyes met Nell's over the rim of her coffee-cup for a second, then the secretary put down her cup.

'Well, I'm not,' she said bluntly. 'When Liz told me Jonah

and his friends were doing some sort of tribute to Elvis—I'm sorry, but…'

'I know.' Nell nodded. 'Major embarrassment moment on the horizon.'

'It's not that I don't like Elvis,' Fiona continued, 'but he's so not Jonah, is he? Jonah's… He's more of an Arran sweater, corduroy trousers and folk songs sort of guy, isn't he?'

'I've tried to talk him out of it, Fiona,' Nell said, 'but he just won't listen.'

'Why should he listen?' Bea protested, glancing from Fiona to Nell, then back again. 'If the man wants to be part of an Elvis tribute band, why shouldn't he be?'

'Because we like Jonah,' Fiona said patiently, 'and it will be mortifying if people laugh at him.'

'Not to mention the fact that he'll never hear the end of it if his act is a disaster,' Nell pointed out, and Bea put down her coffee, her cheeks flushed and angry.

'*If* Jonah's act is a disaster, *if* people make fun of him. Doesn't it occur to either of you that he might actually be bloody good?' the ward sister demanded. 'No, of course it doesn't because you're both so damn blinkered when it comes to Jonah. And Nell, you're the worst.'

'Hey!'

'The man's bright, charming and good-looking,' Bea continued. 'So maybe he's not good-looking in the way Lawrence Summers is, but he's worth ten of the consultant, and yet you constantly underestimate him.'

'I do not!' Nell exclaimed. 'Give me one example of when I've underestimated Jonah.'

'You're doing it now with your assumption that he's going to be rubbish tonight,' Bea said, and Nell coloured.

'OK, maybe that's wrong of me,' she muttered, 'but can you honestly picture Jonah in a tribute band to Elvis and not want to snigger?'

'Yes, I can,' Bea said, 'because, unlike you, I have faith in him.'

'That's a bit unfair,' Fiona protested. 'Nell is Jonah's closest friend.'

'His closest friend?' Bea repeated. 'Nell can't even see what's under her own damn nose.'

'Now, just a minute,' Nell said, her cheeks every bit as red as Bea's now, but Bea didn't give her one.

'I'm going back to Intensive,' the ward sister said. 'The babies in there have more sense than the two of you put together.'

And she banged out of Fiona's office, leaving Nell and Fiona staring, open-mouthed, at one another.

'Well, I have to say that was completely uncalled for,' Fiona said when she'd got her voice back. 'We're only trying to shield Jonah.'

Yes, but why should they believe he needed it? Nell wondered as the secretary went on to mutter darkly about people who put in their pennyworth on the basis of very little knowledge. Why hadn't she and Fiona thought, like Bea, Good for him, when they'd heard Jonah had volunteered to take part in the contest instead of Oh, my God, disaster?

Because the ward sister was right, she realised. They expected him to fail, to look ridiculous, because to them Jonah was just Jonah. A nice man, but not a particularly special sort of a man, and that was wrong, so wrong.

OK, she decided as she finished her coffee and went back into the unit. From now on she was going to stop underestimating Jonah. He would be great in the concert tonight. Wonderful. Sensational.

She hoped.

'Lord, but who would have thought so many people could possess so little talent?' Fiona groaned, as the curtains closed across the stage in the function suite on yet another excruciating act. 'Talk about embarrassing.'

'Arthur Randall from Dentistry wasn't bad,' Nell said, and Fiona's eyebrows hit her hairline.

'You *like* plate spinning?'

'He didn't drop any, he didn't tell corny jokes, and best of all he didn't sing,' Nell said. 'In my book, that puts him well ahead of the competition.'

'Ah, but you haven't seen Jonah yet.' Liz smiled as she slipped into a seat beside them.

'Shouldn't you be backstage with the performers?' Nell said. 'Giving them—' *Giving Jonah.* '—moral support.' Giving Jonah moral support.

'There's only Jonah's act to go and he doesn't need any moral support. He's good.'

Having sat through nineteen acts of varying degrees of awfulness, Nell didn't put much store on the Obs and Gynae sister's ability to be able to judge anything.

'Even so, Liz,' she began. 'Don't you think—'

'Plus I want to be out front to see everyone's reaction,' Liz continued. 'Because, believe me, once the staff see Jonah perform tonight, nobody is ever going to look at him in the same light again.'

That's what I'm afraid of, Nell thought, then plastered an I-just-know-he's-going-to-be-wonderful smile to her lips when she noticed Bea's eyes on her. A smile that didn't prevent her from crossing her fingers and praying when the lights in the function suite dimmed and the curtains in front of the stage slowly opened.

Her first thought as she stared at the three men on the stage was, Thank God they're all wearing ordinary denim jeans and blue shirts. Her second thought was that none of the men was Jonah.

'Do you think he's been paged by the unit?' She whispered in Fiona's ear as the drummer and two guitarists began to play the introduction to 'Jailhouse Rock'.

'Surely somebody would have made an announcement?' Fiona whispered back. 'Done the owing-to-unforeseen-circumstances bit. Perhaps he's…'

'Perhaps he's what?' Nell asked, but Fiona wasn't listening to her.

Somebody had started to sing. Somebody with a dark, raunchy, spine-tingling voice. And as Nell turned towards the sound her mouth fell open.

There, on the stage, bathed in a spotlight, was Jonah, but it wasn't the Jonah she knew. The Jonah she knew was every woman's big brother. A non-sexual shoulder to cry on, a pal, a mate, whereas this Jonah…

This Jonah was gyrating his hips in a way that would have got him arrested if he'd done it on a public highway. This Jonah was wearing a white shirt open to the waist and skin-tight leather trousers that left almost nothing to the imagination.

'Wow, but he won't ever be embarrassed in the showers, will he?' Fiona said, sounding slightly strangled, and Nell shook her head.

'Do you reckon he's naturally hairless?' Bea breathed. 'Or do you think he shaved his chest for tonight?'

Nell didn't know. All she did know was that Jonah's open shirt should have been the worst cliché in the world, but wasn't. Not when the shirt in question revealed a smooth, broad, glistening chest that simply screamed out to be touched, caressed.

'He…he's got a very good voice,' Nell managed to say when Jonah came to the end of 'Jailhouse Rock' and launched without stopping into 'Blue Suede Shoes'.

'He's got a very good everything,' Fiona said, fanning herself with her programme.

'Fiona, you're a happily married woman!' Nell exclaimed.

'So are half the women in the audience,' Fiona protested, 'and they can't believe what they're seeing either.'

Fiona was right. One glance at the serried rows of slack jaws around Nell told her that every woman in the audience was thinking the same thing. When had Jonah Washington become such a hunk? It wasn't like he came in to work dressed the way he was dressed tonight, but never could anyone have imagined that his white coat would hide what it had obviously been hiding. A sexy, gorgeous, male hunk.

'Told you you'd be impressed, didn't I?' Liz shouted as Jonah came to the end of 'Blue Suede Shoes' and the audience erupted in a cacophony of wolf whistles, cheers and shouts for more.

Impressed wasn't the word she would have used, Nell thought. Stunned would have been more accurate.

'The head of Pharmacy's certainly impressed,' Bea observed. 'She's just thrown her business card on the stage.'

'She hasn't,' Nell gasped, craning forward in her seat. But she had, and other cards were being thrown now, swirling around the stage like jumbo confetti.

Lord, but it was going to be knickers next, she thought with a gulp, but it wasn't. Jonah swiftly changed the tempo and instead of another bouncy rock-and-roll number he began to sing the slow ballad, 'Are you Lonesome tonight?' Gradually the wolf whistles died away, and by the time he'd reached the second verse Nell knew that each and every woman in the audience felt as though he was singing this song just for her.

She felt it, too, but as she sat and listened to him it wasn't pleasure she felt. It was horror. Horror because she knew now with blinding clarity that the odd feelings she'd been experiencing in his company hadn't been due to stress, or palpitations, or muddled emotions. It had been lust she'd felt. Lust, and longing, but how could she feel that way about him, about any man, when less than three weeks ago she'd been engaged to Brian? What kind of woman was she that she could so quickly forget the man she'd once sworn undying love to?

'There's no doubt who's won, is there?' Bea exclaimed, as Jonah came to the end of the song and the function suite erupted again, with every female member of staff on their feet cheering.

'No,' Nell muttered, and there wasn't.

Liz shot away, and within five minutes she emerged, red-cheeked and flustered, on the stage with Cynthia Braithwaite, Olivia Hardcastle and Lawrence Summers to proclaim Jonah the winner. Nobody heard who came second and third over the cheers, and nobody cared.

'Let's go backstage and congratulate him,' Fiona said, after Olivia had presented Jonah with the ugliest statuette Nell had ever seen while Lawrence stood to one side, looking as though there was a bad smell under his nose.

'Jonah will be tired, Fiona,' Nell protested, but the secretary wasn't listening.

Determinedly she clasped Nell and Bea by the arm and towed them out of the function suite and down the corridor.

'We're obviously not the only ones who want to congratulate him.' Bea laughed when they reached backstage to find at least thirty nurses giggling and chattering outside the boiler room, which had been converted into a makeshift changing room for the night.

'No, but we're the only ones who are members of his staff,' Fiona declared, elbowing her way through the throng. 'And who has more right than us to be here?'

Mary-Anne for a start, Nell realised when Jonah's girlfriend opened the door and let them in, closing the door again quickly to keep out the crush of excited nurses.

'Phew, but I always thought nurses were a polite, reserved bunch,' the girl gasped, 'but that lot out there... Thank goodness there's another exit or I don't think I'd get Jonah out in one piece.'

'Jonah, you were absolutely incredible!' Fiona exclaimed, walking towards him and giving him a hug. 'Wasn't he incredible, Bea?'

'Stupendous,' Bea declared, and she hugged him, too, and Nell kept her hands firmly to her sides and stared at the floor.

'What did you think of the show, Nell?' Jonah asked.

'You were terrific,' she said simply.

'Really?'

She nodded, but she couldn't meet his gaze, didn't want to meet his gaze. Didn't want to find herself experiencing those feelings of longing all over again. The feelings that would only prove how shallow and superficial she was. That the love she'd thought, had been so sure she'd felt for Brian, had been nothing but a sham.

'We're going on to the Casio Antonio for dinner,' Fiona continued. 'Would the two of you like to come along with us to celebrate your success?'

For a moment Jonah stared at Nell, then shook his head.

'It's been a long day so, if you don't mind, can we take a rain-check?'

'Of course.' Fiona beamed, and as the secretary turned towards the boiler room door Nell beat her through it by a mile.

'Happy now, are you?' Mary-Anne said the minute she and Jonah were alone, and Jonah rolled his eyes with exasperation.

'Mary-Anne, if you're going to start on at me again—'

'You're beginning to enjoy this, aren't you?' his sister interrupted. 'Nell not knowing whether she's coming or going, all those women out there baying for your blood.'

'I don't think it's my blood they're interested in,' Jonah said, his brown eyes dancing, and Mary-Anne shook her head.

'That's what I mean. You're enjoying this—and to think you had the nerve to tell Nell to remember people have feelings. She has feelings, too, Jonah.'

'Sis—'

'Can't you see that what you're doing is wrong, and not just wrong but it could backfire on you big time?' Mary-Anne demanded. 'Think about it, Jonah. Nell clearly believes your story that we're an item, but is she the kind of girl who would try to break us up? No, I didn't think she was,' his sister continued when Jonah opened his mouth, then closed it again. 'And if she won't try to break us up, what happens now?'

'I…I haven't thought that far ahead,' he murmured.

In truth, he hadn't thought about it at all. All he'd wanted was for Nell to see he was a man, with a man's feelings, desires, and he'd just assumed that somehow, some way, everything would work itself out.

'Well, I have thought,' Mary-Anne declared, 'and all I can see is trouble ahead so either you tell Nell the truth about me or I will.'

'But—'

'I mean it, Jonah,' his sister continued. 'I'll give you a week to tell Nell I'm your sister, but that's all. And now I'm going to wait in the car,' she continued, as he tried to interrupt. 'Because if I don't, I'm going to hit you.'

And before he could reply his sister had swung out of the room, leaving him staring in exasperation after her.

'Women,' he muttered out loud to the empty room.

He couldn't deny he'd enjoyed seeing Nell becoming increasingly hot and bothered these past couple of weeks. Hell, he wouldn't have been human if he hadn't felt a certain satisfaction, and as for the reaction of the Belfield staff tonight, well, every man had an ego, didn't he? But now his sister was threatening to pull the plug on him.

A week. All he had was a week, but he could achieve a lot in a week if he was careful.

A momentary qualm assailed him when he pictured himself telling Nell the truth about Mary-Anne. It had been tough enough this morning when he'd been forced to make up excuses for his sister's behaviour with Lawrence, but if he made what he'd done sound like a harmless joke he was sure Nell would see the funny side of it.

Or tear you limb from limb, his mind whispered, but he crushed down the thought quickly.

Nell had always possessed a good sense of humour, and Mary-Anne was simply overreacting when she'd said that Nell would feel hurt. If he explained it to her properly, made her see that he'd done it for both their benefits, he was sure that everything would work out just fine.

CHAPTER SEVEN

'THAT has to be the tenth female member of staff who's been up to the unit this morning on some feeble pretext or other, and none of them fooled me for a second,' Fiona said with disgust as she watched the disappointed nurse from Occupational Therapy slope off towards the elevators. 'It's Jonah. They all want to see Jonah.'

'I'd have thought they'd have seen more than enough of him last night,' Nell said, trying to keep her voice light, dismissive, and Fiona laughed.

'That was a shocker and a half, wasn't it? Who would have thought our Jonah was hiding all that…that talent under his white coat?'

'Not us, for certain,' Nell murmured.

And definitely not me, she thought as she took the stack of letters Fiona was holding out to her and walked quickly away before the secretary could prolong the conversation or ask her if she was feeling all right because she looked terrible this morning.

She knew she looked terrible. Her own mirror had told her how awful she looked, but she never looked good if she didn't get enough sleep and last night she'd scarcely slept at all. Every time she'd closed her eyes images of Jonah had crowded into her mind. Images of him looking pensively at her, images of him smiling at her and images of him holding out his arms to her in a way he'd never done in real life. Desperately, she'd tried to conjure up Brian's face, to block out Jonah's, but no matter how hard she'd tried, Brian's face had remained elusive, and it terrified the hell out of her. Terrified her because it meant she could no longer trust her own feelings, could no longer be sure that when she said 'I love you' to a man, she actually meant it.

'Sister Nell!'

With an effort she turned to see a young woman in a dressing gown standing at the end of the corridor, and frowned slightly.

'You don't remember me, do you?' the girl continued with a smile, and Nell began to shake her head then her eyes lit up.

'Louise Young,' she said. 'Son's name Simon, born twelve weeks premature last year?'

'Got it in one, Sister, but it was two years ago and, no, I can't believe it either.' The girl laughed when Nell gasped. 'It seems like no time at all, does it? And now Simon has a baby brother. A baby brother who was just as eager to come into the world as Simon was.'

'Your new baby's in the unit?' Nell said, and Louise nodded.

'I went into labour three weeks early with David at four o'clock this morning. Dr Jonah did warn me after Simon was born that there was a twenty to forty per cent risk of my next baby being premature, and he was right.'

'Only by three weeks,' a familiar deep voice declared, and the smile on Nell's face died.

On her list of people to avoid at all costs this morning, Jonah came right at the top. Why couldn't he have phoned in sick today? Any other man would have spent last night celebrating his triumph, been fit for nothing this morning, least of all work, but not Jonah. Here he was, as large as life and twice as cheerful, and for the first time in her life his cheerfulness irritated the hell out of her.

What right had he to be so cheerful when he was the sole cause of her sleepless night? What right had he to stand there looking like a walking advertisement for the great outdoors when she looked like something the cat had dragged in? There was no justice in the world, absolutely none.

'I'll leave the two of you to it, shall I?' she said, beginning to back up the corridor, but to her dismay Louise followed her and so did Jonah.

'I hear you won the hospital talent contest last night with your impersonation of Elvis Presley, Doctor,' Louise said. 'Everybody in Maternity was talking about it, saying how incredible you were.'

'I'd take what Maternity said with a very large pinch of salt, Louise,' Jonah replied, and Nell only just suppressed her huff of disbelief.

Self-deprecation didn't suit him. Not any more. It might have done yesterday when he had been mild-mannered Specialist Registrar Jonah Washington, but not after last night when he'd revealed himself to be actually sizzling-hot Jonah Washington.

'What part of the unit is your son in, Louise?' Nell said, deliberately changing the conversation.

'Special Care. Maternity said they transferred him down here, just to be on the safe side, but you know what that means.'

'In this case, it means exactly what they said,' Jonah said gently. 'David's a good weight—5 pounds 12 ounces—so I don't think he'll be with us long.'

'How long is long, Doctor?' Louise said, and Jonah shook his head.

'You should know me better than that, Louise.'

And I don't know you at all, Nell thought as she stared at him. She'd thought she did. She'd also thought she'd known Brian, but now it seemed she didn't know anything with any certainty any more, and she would have given anything to have her old certainties back. The certainty that Jonah was nothing but a good friend. The certainty that she loved Brian, and he loved her. Those certainties had kept her safe, kept her grounded, whereas now—now all she felt was confusion and bewilderment.

'I'm sorry, Louise, but you'll have to excuse me,' she said quickly. 'I'm afraid I...I have things to do.'

'No problem, Sister.' The girl smiled. 'I know how busy you always are.'

Jonah clearly didn't because, to Nell's dismay, he didn't stay and talk to Louise as she'd hoped. Instead, he fell into step beside her.

'I think Louise's son will probably be able to go home next week,' he said in an undertone. 'At the moment his BP and temperature are normal, and though he's breathing a little fast, it's not too fast for a baby who only made his appearance in the world six hours ago. If he can feed without reflux, and his X-rays and scans show no abnormalities, I'd say we're looking at discharge some time next week, but I didn't want to raise Louise's hopes in case I had to dash them.'

'No,' Nell said, keeping her eyes fixed firmly ahead of her and willing him to go away.

'Ian Moffat is coming in to see me on Monday afternoon,' he continued. 'He tried to worm his way out of it when I telephoned him, pitched me a whole load of rubbish as to why he couldn't come in, but I insisted so it'll be interesting to see what excuses he comes up with for not visiting Tommy.'

Nell shot him a quick glance. 'Jonah, I'd go easy on Ian if I were you. There might be some entirely plausible reason for him not visiting his son.'

'Such as what?' Jonah demanded.

If she was honest, Nell couldn't actually think of anything, and neither did she want to prolong the conversation.

'I'll see you later, then,' she said, opening the door of her office, only to see Jonah take a step forward.

'I don't suppose there's any chance of a coffee?'

He wanted a coffee? As in her making it for him, then him sitting and drinking it in her ten by eight foot office, which always seemed too small when he was there at the best of times? He had to be kidding.

'Sorry, but I'm just dropping off these letters,' she lied, walking smartly into her office and plonking them down on her desk. 'And then I have to…to check on the situation in Transitional.'

'I'll come with you.'

Was he being deliberately obtuse? Why couldn't he just take the hint and go back to his consulting room and stay out of her way for the rest of the day? For the rest of her life would be even better.

'On second thoughts,' she said, 'maybe I should check the files for the unit with Bea. I don't want Gabriel to find any errors when he gets back from his honeymoon.'

'Would you like me to help you with them?' Jonah suggested. 'Three people working on them will get them finished in less than half the time.'

They would, but couldn't he see she felt awkward and uncomfortable in his company, that their old easygoing relationship had gone? Evidently not, because he was smiling at her with his familiar lopsided grin, clearly completely oblivious to what she was thinking and feeling.

'Thanks for the offer,' she said tightly, 'but I'm sure Bea and I will manage fine.'

Quickly she turned on her heel, but not quickly enough because his hand shot out and stayed her.

'Nell, if I didn't know better, I'd say you were trying to avoid me.'

Finally, the penny had dropped, she thought, but she couldn't say that.

'Of course I'm not avoiding you,' she said instead, all apparent surprise that he could even suggest such a thing. 'I just know how very busy you are, and I didn't want to take up your time.'

He nodded slowly but he didn't look convinced. He looked bewildered. Bewildered and confused, and rumpled, and, oh, so desirable, and as his eyes met hers, and her heart did a little tango, she gritted her teeth. Somehow she had to get her emotions under control. If he ever found out what she was thinking and feeling, it would be completely humiliating.

'Look, I'm sorry,' she said awkwardly. 'I'm being really snarky today, aren't I? And it's not your fault.' Like hell it wasn't, but the situation called for damage limitation, not confrontation. 'If you want to help Bea and me with the files, that would be great.'

A smile lit up his face. There were still traces of lurking confusion in his eyes, but at least she'd defused the situation for the moment and, as she walked down the corridor and into Intensive Care to find Bea, she could only pray that something in there would distract him.

It didn't. For a stricken hour and a half she, Bea and Jonah ploughed their way through the files of the babies who had been in the unit when Gabriel had left for his honeymoon, cross-checking them against the files of the babies who had since come in and those who had been discharged. It should have been boring, tedious, and it would have been if Bea's office hadn't been even smaller than her own.

'It's just as well we're all such good friends.' Bea laughed when Jonah squeezed past Nell for the umpteenth time to retrieve something from the filing cabinet.

'I'm not doing it intentionally,' Jonah protested. 'It's just that most of the files are in the cabinet beside Nell.'

'Relax!' Bea exclaimed. 'I'm only kidding, aren't I, Nell?'

Nell muttered something in reply, but she didn't know what. All she did know was if she didn't get out of this room soon, she was going to lose what little remained of her sanity.

'I think we should call it a day,' she said. 'We're more than halfway through the files, and it'll soon be time for Jonah's morning round.'

'Will it?' he said with apparent surprise. 'Goodness, doesn't time fly when you're having fun?'

He might be, Nell thought, shutting the filing cabinet drawer beside her with a bang, but she sure as hell wasn't.

'Your morning round,' she said pointedly, and he grinned at her.

A grin that made her wonder just how many of his trips to the filing cabinet had been strictly necessary, and whether he could possibly have suspected what she was thinking, feeling, and had decided to capitalise on it?

Unconsciously, she shook her head as they all trooped out of Bea's office and into Intensive Care. Jonah wouldn't do that. He wasn't a manipulator, a player of games, neither did he lie. She'd stake her life on that.

'Oh, dear, Megan Thornton doesn't look any happier today,' Bea murmured.

'There's a problem?' Nell asked, her professional instincts kicking in immediately.

'Not a problem as such,' the ward sister replied. 'I just happened to mention to her yesterday that if Adam keeps improving we might be able to move him back into Special soon, and I'm afraid she's quite stressed about it.'

'A lot of mums and dads react that way,' Nell observed. 'I suppose it's because they start off being terrified of all the high-tech equipment, then they realise it's what's keeping their babies alive, and when we tell them we're going to withdraw it...' he shrugged '...they panic.'

'I'd better have a word with her,' Jonah said, and as he walked off across the unit, Nell let out a sigh of relief.

A sigh that was short-lived because, try as she may, she couldn't stop her eyes following him.

When had she become attracted to him? *Why* had she become attracted to him? If she looked at him calmly, dispassionately, she could see that he was actually rather a good-looking man. He was also kind, and thoughtful, and compassionate, but why hadn't she seen any of that before, or was she perhaps not so much attracted to him as simply trying to fill the vacuum that Brian had left in her life?

One thing was certain. He was never, ever going to know how

she felt. From now she was going to be coolly distant. Polite, but distant, because there was safety in distance.

'Sister Nell?'

She turned to see Tricia Kelly standing behind her, and hitched a smile to her lips.

'Something I can help you with, Tricia?' she said.

'I was just wondering—I know it's silly—but the heating, and oxygen, and all the wires and tubes Katie needs. What happens if there's a power failure?'

'We have back-up generators, which switch on immediately,' Nell replied. 'Plus each individual incubator is fitted with its own set of alarms, so if there's a problem with one incubator's temperature or oxygen supply, an alarm will alert us.'

And that wasn't what was really worrying Tricia, she thought as she stared at her, but she had been an NICU nurse long enough to know there were times when you pushed for information, and times when you waited, and this was one of the waiting times.

'Is that a new teddy bear for Katie?' she said, seeing the soft toy peeping out of Tricia's shopping bag.

'One of the girls at work gave it to me, and Sister Bea said it would be all right to bring it in just so long as I didn't mind it being wrapped in plastic to guard against infection.' Tricia took the bear out of her bag, then bit her lip. 'I was hoping…I thought we were supposed to get Katie's eye test results back today, Sister. '

Deliberately, Nell avoided looking in Jonah's direction. Tricia's voice was low but Jonah had ears like a bat and she knew he would have heard what the woman had said.

'There's still time, Tricia,' she said gently, and saw tears glisten in Tricia's eyes.

'My husband went on the internet last night, looking for things that could happen to premature babies' eyes, and he found all these articles on retinopathy of prematurity.'

Oh, hell, there were times when Nell wished the internet had never been invented, or medical books, or any of the in-depth medical programmes that never seemed to be off the television. A little knowledge was most definitely a dangerous thing.

'Tricia—'

'Rob's mother went blind in her sixties, and he said he wouldn't wish that on his worst enemy.'

'Tricia, we're not going to know anything until Mr Brentwood has completed his diagnosis,' Nell said. 'So do, please, try not to worry.'

Which was a stupid thing to say, and she knew it was, but she wasn't a qualified ophthalmologist, and until Mr Braithwaite got back to them they were all playing a waiting game.

But not for much longer. Jonah had just finished his morning round when Bea whispered something to him and he disappeared out of Intensive.

'Something wrong?' Nell asked, and Bea grimaced ruefully.

'Mr Brentwood's arrived.'

'And?'

'He wasn't smiling,' Bea replied, 'but, then, he's never a barrel of laughs, is he?'

The consultant wasn't, and neither was he a speedy talker because it was a good forty-five minutes before Jonah returned.

'Well?' Nell murmured as she walked towards him.

'I've just phoned Rob Kelly to ask him to come in so we can discuss Katie's results with him and his wife,' he said. 'Will you be able to sit in with us?'

Nell nodded. 'Not a problem.' She searched his face. 'Is the news bad?'

'As bad as it can be,' he said grimly.

'But you said she was doing so well,' Tricia protested. 'Only last week you said you'd never known a ten-and-a-half-week preemie come on as well as Katie has.'

'Tricia—'

'Even on Monday, when Mr Brentwood said he'd like to

etest her eyes,' Tricia continued as though Jonah hadn't spoken,
you didn't say anything, didn't even give us the smallest hint
that something might be wrong.'

And that would teach him to be the big I-know-it-all specialist registrar, Jonah thought as he glanced across at Nell to see
she was staring at the calendar on his consulting-room wall as
though it was the most riveting thing she'd ever seen.

'I'm so sorry, Tricia.' Deliberately he avoided looking across
at Nell again. 'Somebody told me I should warn you there might
be a problem, but I thought, hoped, we wouldn't need to have
this conversation.'

'Well, we're having it now,' Rob said with a bluster Jonah
knew was merely a mask to hide his devastation. 'And what I
want to know is, when Mr Brentwood says Katie is blind, does
he mean there's no operation, no treatment that could restore
Katie's sight?'

Jonah shifted uncomfortably in his seat. He hated being put
on the spot like this, hated having to dash parents' hopes, but he
also knew that he couldn't lie.

'I'm afraid there isn't,' he said with difficulty. 'The damage
to her retinas is too extensive.'

A sob broke from Tricia, and she searched fruitlessly in her
handbag for a handkerchief.

'Why couldn't she have been deaf?' she asked. 'If she'd been
deaf she could still have got about, managed to be independent, but
to be blind, to live in a world of darkness like Rob's mother. And
Katie's so little. She has a whole lifetime of blindness ahead of her.'

'Blindness isn't a death sentence, Tricia,' Jonah began, only
to pause as Nell quickly scooped the box of tissues off his desk
and handed it to Tricia.

Hell, he should have done that. Why hadn't he done that? He
was usually first off the mark when practical help was required,
but today his brain felt fuzzy, woolly.

Because half of it is thinking about Nell, a little voice whispered at the back of his head, and it shouldn't be. He should be concentrating on his job, but she was acting so weirdly today. Maybe she had PMT. Maybe she just hadn't slept very well last night. She certainly didn't look as though she'd slept. There were dark shadows under her eyes, and her face looked drawn and pinched.

'This Brentwood man,' Rob said, his voice gruff as his wife wiped her cheeks with one of the paper hankies, then blew her nose. 'Is he any good at his job? I mean, people make mistakes, give the wrong diagnosis, and how can he possibly tell whether Katie is able to see or not? She's not even three weeks old so he can hardly hold up a card and say to her, "Is this a ball, or a flower?", can he?'

'The tests Mr Brentwood uses are based on him examining the structure and formation of the various parts of Katie's eyes,' Jonah replied gently. 'From these tests he can ascertain whether her eyes are capable of sight, and in his opinion they're not. We can certainly arrange for another ophthalmologist to examine Katie, but Mr Brentwood is a very highly experienced consultant and I have to say I don't think there's any possibility of him making a mistake.'

Rob cleared his throat noisily. 'Right. Just thought I'd ask, make sure, in case there might be, you know, some doubt.'

Jonah wished there was. He wished even more that he wasn't having this conversation with the couple, but he knew he couldn't avoid it. Knew, too, that breaking bad news was part of his job, but knowing that fact never made it any easier.

'Mr Brentwood would like to perform laser surgery on Katie's eyes,' he continued. 'He can't restore her sight, but what he'd like to do is to try to save as much of Katie's retinas as he can so that if some new procedure becomes available in the future, what he can save now might possibly be utilised. It's not a dangerous or serious operation, and Katie will be fully recovered from it within forty-eight hours.'

The couple nodded, but he knew they weren't listening to him. All they'd heard since he'd broken the bad news to them was the word 'blind'.

'Well, I really screwed that up big time, didn't I?' he said bleakly, after the couple had signed the consent forms for laser surgery, then made their excuses and left. 'I should have listened to you, forewarned them about the possibilities, but, no, I was the big-cheese acting consultant who knew best, wasn't I?'

'You did what you thought you should, Jonah,' Nell said softly, and he shook his head.

'Did I?' he said. 'Did I really, or was I just too plain arrogant, too certain that I was right and you were wrong?'

'I don't think it's a question of right or wrong,' Nell said. 'You were trying to shield the Kellys from two days of worry and fear. Maybe that's not what I would have done but, then, I'm a glass half-empty sort of a person, and you're a glass half-full one.'

'Complete opposites, in fact. But, then, you know what they say about opposites,' he added, his lips curving into a smile, but no answering smile came from her.

In fact, Nell's face was positively stony as she replied, 'I've always thought that was a particularly stupid saying.'

O-kay, Jonah thought as he stared at her. So it hadn't been his imagination earlier. He was in the doghouse for some reason, and he could either ignore it, or confront it head on, and seeing how badly he'd screwed up using avoidance tactics with the Kellys, this time he was going for the head-on approach.

'I give up,' he said.

'Sorry?' she said, looking completely startled, but at least he'd got her to look at him. 'Give up on what?'

'Trying to figure out what I've done to annoy you,' he said, affixing what he hoped was his most appealing smile to his face. 'It's obviously something mega, so why don't you just tell me what it is so I can apologise and then we can be friends again?'

He expected her to laugh. The Nell he'd known for the past

two years would have laughed, but this Nell didn't. This Nell looked if anything, even frostier than before.

'You haven't done anything,' she said.

'I must have.'

'You haven't.'

'I obviously have.'

'Jonah, you haven't annoyed me, irritated me, or done anything that I've taken umbrage at,' she said, the irritation in her voice completely belying her words, 'so can we please just drop this subject?'

She was getting to her feet. She was leaving. And he didn't want her to leave, so he said the first thing that came into his head.

'Are you still angry with me because I yelled at you on Monday?'

'No, of course I'm not,' she protested, but as he watched a hot tide of colour creep across her cheeks he knew he'd hit the nail right on the head.

Or if not the exact nail, he'd obviously come pretty close to it, which meant her coolness had something to do with Mary-Anne, and he swore under his breath. His sister had been right. This had gone on long enough. All he was doing was digging himself into an ever-deepening hole, and somehow he had to get himself out of it.

'Nell, about Mary-Anne—'

'Jonah, I really don't want to hear this,' Nell interrupted, agitation plain on her face. 'I don't feel comfortable talking about your private life.'

Neither did he, but, then, he knew what she didn't. That his so-called private life was nothing but a lie, a sham, a fraud.

'Nell—'

'Jonah, please. Your private life is really none of my business.'

'Isn't it?'

Her eyes met his, then skittered away fast. Oh, hell, she couldn't have looked more uncomfortable if he'd walked in on her in her bath. He had to tell her the truth, but what if he told her the truth and she didn't see the funny side of it? What if—and this would be ten times worse—she simply didn't care? For sure, he thought she seemed a lot more aware of him as a man than she had been before, but awareness didn't mean she was attracted to him, and if he told her the truth, and she didn't care, what then?

But do you really want your sister to tell her? a little voice in his head asked. And she will, you know she will, and you've only got a week. Six days now, to be exact.

'Nell…' He picked up one of the pens on his desk and put it down again. 'Have you ever done something you bitterly regret? Something that you did with the best of intentions, the very best of motivations, but…' he moved his shoulders awkwardly …something you see later was not just foolhardy but plain dumb?'

The agitation on her face disappeared. 'Jonah, if you're still thinking about Katie…'

'I'm not talking about Katie,' he interrupted. 'I was meaning on a…a personal level.'

'Oh.' She was uncomfortable again. He could see it in her body language, in the way she wasn't meeting his gaze. 'I don't… I mean, I can't immediately think of anything,' she replied, 'but I guess we've all managed to screw something up at one time or another.'

'Exactly.' He nodded, feeling a trickle of sweat run down his back. *Say it, Jonah. Get it over with. Tell her.* 'You see, the thing is… Mary-Anne and I…We're… She's… She's not…'

'Not what?'

Oh, double hell. Why had he ever got himself into this mess? he wondered. It had been a really dumb plan that was never going to work. It was always going to end in disaster, and he should have thought it through, realised where it could lead.

'Mary-Anne,' he began again. 'She isn't… She and I aren't…'

'Aren't what?'

Oh, hell. Nell was looking at him oddly now, probably wondering when he was going to get to the point. Or thinking he'd lost it entirely.

'Mary-Anne and I... I—I've decided you were right,' he said in a rush. 'She's not the girl for me. It's over.'

There, it was done. He hadn't told Nell the whole truth, but at least he wouldn't have to keep on pretending that his sister was his girlfriend any more.

'I'm sorry.'

'You are?' he said faintly. Damn it, she wasn't supposed to be sorry, she was supposed to be glad.

'I'm always sorry if somebody's relationship fails,' Nell murmured. 'Having been there myself, I know how very painful it can be.'

'Right.' He nodded. 'But these things happen, and you have to move on, don't you?'

'Yes.'

'Nell—'

'I really do have to go, Jonah,' she interrupted. 'It's way past time for me to check on the nursing staff.'

She was leaving, and to his dismay she still didn't look any happier. Maybe expecting her to beam with pleasure at his news that he and Mary-Anne had broken up had been a little over-optimistic, but he'd expected something more than just sympathy.

Of course she was going to be sympathetic, he told himself. Nell's a generous, kind-hearted woman. She's not the sort to immediately think, Terrific, Mary-Anne's out of the picture. She'll want to give you time to recover emotionally.

From what? his mind demanded. *You've lied again.*

He groaned as he got to his feet and went to stare out of his consulting-room window. He might have dug himself out of one hole, but he'd gone and dug himself into another one. Now he was going to have to play the heartbroken man for a few weeks or Nell would think he was shallow, superficial, and that wasn't what he wanted at all. If only he'd told her how he'd felt two years ago, but he hadn't, and it was all because of Rowan. Rowan, who had been exactly the kind of girl Nell feared Mary-Anne was.

She'd been so pretty, he remembered. Pretty, and lively, and full of fun, and when his friends had tried to warn him he'd thought they'd simply been jealous, envious. He'd had to find out the hard way that Rowan had been more interested in his burgeoning career than she had been in him as a man, and so when he'd first met Nell he'd been running scared. Scared that he would be hurt again, and scared that having got it so spectacularly wrong with Rowan he could no longer trust his ability to judge whether somebody was lying to him or not.

'Fool,' he murmured out loud. 'Stupid, stupid fool.'

'At last, some self-knowledge.'

His head jerked round, and panic flooded through him as he saw his sister standing in the doorway of his consulting room.

'You said I had a week to tell Nell,' he said. 'I distinctly remember you saying I had a week.'

'Relax, big bro.' Mary-Anne smiled. 'I left my scarf at the hospital last night and I only came by to see if anyone had handed it in.'

'This isn't the lost and found department, Mary-Anne,' he said more sharply than he'd intended, and his sister's eyebrows rose.

'I also thought I'd say hi to you while I was here, but that was clearly a mistake. I'll go back and talk to that nice girl on reception.'

She half turned to go, and Jonah shot after her.

'You've been talking to Fiona?' he exclaimed. 'Who else have you talked to?'

'Who else?' His sister look infuriatingly thoughtful. 'Well, there was a very nice porter on the ground floor, then that very nice doctor in the elevator…'

'Mary-Anne.'

'If you mean Nell—and I'm sure you do—I've neither see her nor talked to her. Look, Jonah,' his sister continued, as he le out an audible sigh of relief, 'if you would only just tell her th truth, you wouldn't have a heart attack every time I appeared.'

'I have told her. Sort of,' he added in an undertone, but he' forgotten what sharp ears Mary-Anne had.

'What do you mean, *sort of*?' she demanded. 'How can yo *sort of* tell somebody the truth?'

'I told her….' He felt his cheeks redden. 'I told her I'd decide we weren't right for one another, and that we'd split up.'

'Heaven give me strength.' Mary-Anne groaned. 'Jonah just how serious are you about Nell? I mean, what are yo wanting here?'

Jonah stared down at his hands. 'I…I love her, sis, and if…; she could ever feel the same way about me…'

'You'd want to marry her?' she finished for him, and whe he nodded, she straightened up. 'Then she's going to want t meet your family at some time in the future, isn't she? And I'm telling you now I'm not spending your entire married life hidin in case she recognises me.'

'It's…it's difficult, Mary-Anne,' he said awkwardly, and sh gave him a how-can-this-idiot-be-my-brother look.

'I warned you that you were digging yourself into a hole didn't I?'

'So now you're going to gloat?'

'Now I'm saying sort it, Jonah, and do it fast.'

'I was trying to,' he protested, 'but she's behaving so oddl today. It's like…' He shook his head. 'We've always got on s well together, but she's been avoiding me—I know she has—an when we meet she doesn't look me in the eye any more.'

'Of course she doesn't,' Mary-Anne said in exasperatio 'because having seen her last night, I'd say your crazy plan ha actually worked, and now she's feeling guilty.'

'Why should she feel guilty?' Jonah demanded, astonishment plain on his face, and his sister gave him a pitying look.

'Because she'll be wondering how she could possibly be in love with one man one minute, promise to marry him, then find herself suddenly attracted to somebody else.'

'But if you're right—and I'm not one hundred per cent certain you are—can't she just see she made a mistake with Brian?' Jonah protested. 'Admit what she thought was love wasn't love after all?'

'Jonah, she lived with Brian for a year. That's a hell of a big mistake for a woman to make. She's going to have to work it through, come to terms with it.'

'Oh.'

'Yup. "Oh", big bro.' Mary-Anne nodded. 'And I have to say I don't much fancy your chances of coming out of this mess unscathed. Not after you tell her I'm your sister, and she discovers you've lied to her not once but twice.'

CHAPTER EIGHT

OH, HELL, Jonah thought as he sat in his consulting room and stared at Tommy Moffat's father. Nell had told him to take it easy, warned him there could be a perfectly plausible reason for Ian's failure to visit his son, but he hadn't listened. He'd just stormed in, all guns blazing, and now he felt like a heel. The biggest heel of all time, with the added bonus of knowing he only had himself to blame.

'I'm so very sorry, Ian,' he murmured. 'I just wish you'd told me this before. If you'd only told me, or if Helen had.'

'She doesn't know how I feel, Doctor,' Ian interrupted. 'You see, she was so pleased when she discovered she was pregnant and I thought everything would be all right, and then she went into labour early, and Tommy was so very small...'

'Ian—'

'We're supposed to be the strong ones, aren't we, Doctor?' Ian continued, as though Jonah hadn't spoken. 'Men, I mean. We're not supposed to fall apart so I thought, Keep it to yourself, don't upset Helen when she's so worried about Tommy. 'I do want to visit Tommy, to be here for him.' He shook his head. 'But the minute I walk into the unit, smell the antiseptic, I...'

Jonah wasn't surprised. He wouldn't have wanted to go anywhere near the Belfield Infirmary either if his first wife had died there, giving birth to a baby boy. A boy who had died just five weeks later in the neonatal intensive care unit.

'Ian, would you like me to make you an appointment to see one of our psychiatrists?' he suggested. 'I'm not saying you need psychiatric help,' Jonah added quickly, as dark colour suffused Ian's thin cheeks, 'but sometimes after the death of a loved one people are left with unresolved issues, and speaking to an outsider, somebody who's not a family member or a friend, can be helpful.'

And maybe he himself should think about getting some professional help, too, Jonah thought after Ian had gone. Screwing up with Katie Kelly's parents had been bad enough, but now he'd done it again with Ian, and he never used to be like that. In fact, he'd always prided himself on his ability to read people, interpret situations, but it all seemed to be going wrong, and he didn't know why.

'Ready for your afternoon round, Jonah?'

Nell was hovering awkwardly in his consulting-room doorway, and he managed a small, tight smile.

'Do you want a truthful answer or a sanitised one?'

Her eyebrows rose. 'Monday afternoon blues, or something worse?'

'You've just missed Ian Moffat. He told me…' Jonah cleared his throat. 'He told me his first wife died in the Belfield, giving birth to their son. A son who subsequently died in NICU.'

'Oh, hell!' Nell exclaimed. 'No wonder the poor man hasn't been visiting Tommy. This place must hold such awful memories for him.'

'And I trampled all over his memories with my size-eleven boots,' Jonah said morosely, and a faint smile appeared on Nell's lips.

'I doubt that very much, Jonah.'

'I immediately thought, lousy father, Nell,' he declared, 'and I should never have jumped to that conclusion. You said there might be a plausible reason for his absence, but did I listen? No, not me. Not big-shot, acting consultant Jonah Washington.'

'Jonah—'

'I'm losing it, aren't I?' he said, and Nell stared at him uncertainly for a second then came forward and sat down.

'OK, listen to me, and listen good,' she said. 'You are not losing it. In fact, you've done a wonderful job running the unit in Gabriel's absence.'

'Yeah, right,' he said without conviction, and a slight frown creased her forehead.

'This angsting you're doing. It's because of Katie Kelly, isn't it? You're still feeling guilty about her.'

'I should have warned her parents, Nell,' he said. 'You told me to, but I didn't listen. I just let them go on believing that the repeat eye tests were standard practice, nothing for them to worry about, so when they got the bad news it was all the harder for them to bear.'

'Jonah, what if Katie's eyes had been fine?'

'They weren't,' he said impatiently.

'No, but what if they had been?' Nell asked. 'What if you'd told Rob and Tricia all the horrible things that could be wrong with Katie's eyes, and they spent days worrying about it, and then you bounced up and said, "Sorry, folks. Katie's eyes are actually fine." Would that have been better?'

Jonah opened his mouth, then closed it again. 'I don't know. I guess I did what I thought was right at the time.'

'Exactly.' Nell nodded. 'Jonah, you're not God. You don't know the future. All you can do is work with the cards you're dealt, and sometimes you'll get it right, and sometimes you'll get it wrong.'

'Like I did with Ian Moffat,' he said. 'I got that one wrong big time.'

Nell sat back in her seat. 'OK, what did you say to him?'

'That it was just as important for fathers to visit their children as it was for mothers. That Tommy…' Jonah winced as he remembered. 'That Tommy was a beautiful little boy, and there were men out there who would give their right arms to have him as a son, and yet he was neglecting him.'

'All of which is true.'

'Yes, but—'

'Ian *was* neglecting his son, Jonah. Maybe not for the reasons you assumed, but he *was* neglecting him, and he had to be called on that.'

'I suppose,' Jonah muttered.

'Suppose nothing,' Nell dismissed. 'Jonah, there's no way you could have known Ian's background, and if you hadn't phoned him, made him come in, we would never have found out about it, neither would you have been able to offer him help. And I bet you offered him help, didn't you?'

'I said I could make him an appointment to see one of our psychiatrists.'

'And did he take you up on it?'

'Yes.'

'Then you've helped him, haven't you?' Nell said, and a rueful smile curved Jonah's lips.

'You should have been a lawyer. With you on the defence team, nobody would ever go to prison.'

She smiled. 'Only if I was defending the good guys. And you're one of the good guys, Jonah.'

He laughed.

'Oh, Nell, what would I do without you?' he said, only to see her smile slip away. Hell's teeth, he'd meant it as a compliment, but she clearly hadn't seen it as one. 'Nell—'

'It's getting late, Jonah,' she interrupted. 'If we don't get a move on we'll clash with Audiology's rounds and you know what they're like if they're kept waiting.'

He did, but right now he didn't care.

'Nell, what I said—about not knowing what I'd do without you—I meant it as a compliment.'

'I know you did,' she replied, 'but you really should be starting your afternoon round.'

Which was true, but what he wanted more was to know why, ever since last Thursday, she had been shutting him out, and she had been, he knew she had. As long as he kept his conversation limited to the unit, and the babies, Nell was prepared to talk, but the minute he attempted to make their conversation more personal the shutters went up, and it was driving him crazy.

'She needs space, Jonah,' his sister had said when he'd told her about it. 'She needs time and space to work things out. It's understandable.'

Which sounded fine in theory, but what if his sister was wrong? It was all very well for Mary-Anne to insist Nell was running away from him because she was attracted to him, but he'd seen damn little evidence to support that, and a hell of a lot more to suggest Nell was still in love with Brian.

'Nell—'

'Your afternoon round, Jonah,' she said pointedly, and he only just bit back a colourful oath.

'OK, OK.' He snapped, but as he got to his feet his phone rang, and he rolled his eyes with exasperation. 'That'll be Haematology. I asked them to ring me back to explain why the blood samples we sent down this morning haven't been returned yet.'

'I'll meet you in Special, then, shall I?' Nell replied, already edging her way to the door.

'No. Wait,' he began, but she didn't wait.

She shot out of his room without a backward glance, leaving him with nothing to do but vent his anger on the haematology technician. An action he performed with great gusto and considerable vitriol, but it didn't help. Yelling at a spluttering technician was easy. Getting the woman he wanted to talk to him was proving to be anything but, and he didn't like it. He didn't like it at all.

Neither did Nell as she waited for him in Special Care and tried to look as though she was listening intently to what Bea was saying

Three and a half days of making polite and neutral conversation with Jonah. Three and a half days of successfully distancing herself from him, and she'd thrown it all away in the space of ten minutes. What did it matter if she'd thought he'd looked really dejected when she'd gone to his consulting room? She should simply have reminded him of his ward round but, no, she'd had to feel sorry for him, had to want to help him, had to *get involved*.

'—shame.'

Bea was gazing at her expectantly, and Nell flushed.

'I'm sorry, Bea. What did you just say?'

'That it was a shame about Jonah and Mary-Anne. Do you think they'll get back together?'

'He seems pretty adamant it's over,' Nell replied.

He did, too. Not only had Mary-Anne's photograph gone from his desk, but even the most casual mention of her name was enough to bring a tight, closed expression to his face.

'Well, at least he won't have far to look for another girl-friend,' Bea said, shooting her a swift sideways glance. 'After his Elvis impersonation, there's a queue of girls in the hospital more than willing to take Mary-Anne's place.'

There was, and a month, even a fortnight ago Nell would have found the crowd of eager-eyed nurses who suddenly simply *had* to speak to Jonah really funny, but she didn't find it funny any more. She felt lost, and bewildered, with a permanent lump in her throat that just wouldn't go away.

What would I do without you? he'd said, but he'd meant as a friend, and she wanted...

She didn't know what she wanted. All she knew was that every time she caught sight of him her heart rate sped up. Every time their eyes met the self-same heart launched into a manic tango. Her ability to keep her feelings under control wasn't getting better, it was getting worse, and she didn't know what to do about it.

'Nell, about Jonah—' Bea began, only to break off quickly when he walked towards them.

'Everything all right here?' he asked, glancing from Nell to Bea, then back again.

'Everything's fine.' Bea smiled, and he smiled, and Nell forced her lips into what she hoped was a smile and not the rictus grin of somebody who was losing it completely.

'David Young,' Jonah said, and Bea handed him the notes.

'Obs perfect,' she said. 'Feeding well, putting on weight.'

'Nothing on the X-rays, nothing on the scans,' Jonah murmured as he leafed through David's chart. 'Let's move him to Transitional tomorrow, with a view to discharging him on Saturday.'

'His mother will be relieved,' Bea observed. 'She was telling me yesterday that her first baby spent three months with us.'

'David was only sent down to us by Maternity as a precaution,' Jonah said. 'He could probably have gone home with Louise, but as he was her second preemie Maternity decided to be cautious.'

Why couldn't she be cautious? Nell wondered as Jonah moved on to Adam Thornton's notes. Why couldn't she be sensible? It was Brian she loved. It had to be or why else had she lived with him for a year, why else had she agreed to marry him?

Because you made a mistake? her heart suggested, but if that was true then how was she ever going to be sure that she wasn't making the same mistake again?

'Adam's been doing very well since you transferred him here on Saturday,' Bea said. 'His BP's perfect, as is his heart rate, and he's been spending longer and longer off his ventilator, with no ill effects at all. In fact...' the ward sister looked uncertainly at Jonah '...his mother was wondering whether she could perhaps try feeding him from a bottle when she comes in to visit him this afternoon.'

Jonah turned to Nell. 'What do you think?'

That he had lovely eyes, beautiful eyes, and such a nice smile. No, not that thought, forget that thought. Erase that thought.

'I don't see why she can't,' she said, pulling herself together quickly. 'As Bea said, Adam's been doing really well, and Megan will be thrilled to bits if you say yes.'

Thrilled to bits was the understatement of the year.

'You mean it?' Megan exclaimed, her eyes very bright, when Jonah asked if she would like to try bottle-feeding her son. 'Oh, Doctor, you have no idea how much I've been wanting to do this. I know you said Adam gets all the nutrients he needs through his feeding tube, but to be able to feed him myself, it's like I'm finally going to be able to be a proper mum to him.'

It was what Viv Nicolson had said, Nell remembered as she noticed the young woman watching Megan enviously from across the unit, and when Jonah began explaining to Megan about skin-to-skin-contact bottle-feeding, she slipped across to Callum's mother.

'It'll be your turn soon, Viv,' she said quietly, and the woman sighed.

'You keep saying that, Sister, but the day never arrives.'

'It will,' Nell insisted. 'I know it's hard, waiting, but you want to do what's best for Callum, don't you?'

'Of course I do. It's just…' Viv bit her lip. 'This skin-to-skin-contact thing Megan's doing. It's not that different from ordinary bottle-feeding, is it, apart from her holding her baby right up against her chest?'

'It's pretty much the same,' Nell agreed. 'We don't know why putting your baby against your bare skin seems to improve a preemie's recovery time, but it does. The only thing you need to remember is to make sure your shirt is completely buttoned up over your baby to keep him warm.'

'Right,' Viv muttered, and Nell knew what Viv was thinking—that there was no point in telling her that when she wasn't being allowed to do it—but before she could say anything, Jonah had joined them.

'Cheer up, Viv,' he said. 'It'll be your turn soon.'

'That's what Sister Nell said,' she replied, and Jonah smiled. 'Then listen to Sister Nell. I always do.'

Or he'd like to, he thought sadly as Nell made her excuses

and walked back to Megan Thornton, but she wasn't talking to him right now so that made it kind of difficult.

And the day interminable, he realised when he'd finished his tour of Special Care and went on to Intensive, with Nell at his side, answering him largely in monosyllables.

Why, oh, why had he ever started this? he wondered. He should have been content with Nell's friendship. At least then she'd talked to him, smiled at him, but in wanting more he seemed only to have succeeded in losing everything. And right now he would have given anything to have her friendship back because without it his world was a lonely, empty place.

'You look tired,' Bea said, when he popped into her small office after his shift had ended.

'Feel it, too,' he said ruefully. 'Maybe I'm getting too old for this job.'

'If you are, then we'd better all think of hanging up our stethoscopes.' Bea laughed, but when he didn't join in her laughter she stared at him thoughtfully for a second then said, 'Look, tell me to mind my own business, but have you ever tried telling Nell how you feel?'

'Bea—'

'It's OK,' she said quickly, as he gazed at her in alarm. 'Nobody else knows. I think I've only seen it because I'm new here, and sometimes outsiders see things others don't.'

He sighed.

'Bea, I can't talk to somebody who won't talk back.'

'Try it, Jonah,' Bea insisted.

Which was all very well for the ward sister to say Jonah thought as he walked out of her office and down the corridor but he'd never been good at one-way conversations and that's all he felt he and Nell shared nowadays.

'I'm off home now, Fiona,' he said, seeing the secretary standing outside her office, lost in thought.

'Right,' she murmured.

'Hopefully there'll be no problems,' he continued, 'but the night staff have my telephone number if they need to get in touch.'

'Yes.'

Don't ask, he told himself, as he saw the secretary's frown deepen. Ever since you told her you and Mary-Anne weren't an item any more, she's taken to greeting you with the solicitous, commiserating expression normally reserved for attendants at a funeral, so don't ask because you know it will simply give her another opportunity to do her 'there, there' routine, and you don't need that, not tonight, and quickly he walked towards the elevator, only to pause.

He couldn't do it. He knew he was going to be very, very sorry, but he just couldn't do it, and with a sigh he turned and walked back.

'Fiona, what's wrong?' he asked, and the secretary shook her head.

'Nothing's wrong, exactly, but Nell's left her mobile phone in her office and I'm trying to remember if there's anybody on staff who could take it to her on their way home. I don't suppose it's urgent or anything, but I keep thinking, What if she doesn't have a landline at home? And if she hasn't, what if she has an emergency and needs to contact somebody quickly?'

Nell lived in the West End of Glasgow and he lived in the East End. It would take him a good forty-five minutes to drive across the city, then another forty-five minutes to get home. He was tired, and hungry, and completely cheesed off, and the way Nell had been behaving towards him lately she'd probably take the phone from him with a polite thank you, then just as politely shut the door in his face.

'I'll take it,' he said.

It was odd, Nell decided as she stared at her gleaming furniture and pristinely swept carpet. According to all the articles she'd read in the glossy magazines, her flat should have become a tip after Brian had dumped her, but it had actually never been quite so clean. Unfortunately, without kids or a pet, a thoroughly cleaned flat tended to stay cleaned unless you deliberately went about dropping things, and even for her that would have been a bridge too far. Which meant she had nothing to do that evening except make herself something to eat, watch some mindless television and go to bed.

'Wow, but you really know how to live life on the edge, Nell,' she muttered, as she picked up her cousin Maddie's postcard and read it again.

> *Of all the cities we've been to on our honeymoon, Rome has got to be my favourite. You'd love it, Nell, and I'm sure Brian would, too. It's so romantic, so historic, and as for the shops! Have you set a date yet for your wedding? I've so much to tell you when we get back, and I'm relying on you to keep me up to date with all the news and gossip.*

Well, she'd have plenty of news to tell Maddie, Nell thought with a sigh as she propped the postcard of the Coliseum back up on her mantelpiece. Like the fact she wasn't marrying Brian any more, like Jonah winning the Belfield Infirmary talent contest and the fact that she…

No, she wasn't even going to think about that, far less tell her cousin. She already felt stupid enough, without sharing her stupidity with somebody else. Which was why, when her doorbell rang, she sped down the corridor with relief. So what if it was only a neighbour wanting to borrow some sugar, or to complain about the woman in number 12? It would be a person to talk to. A person who didn't know Jonah, wouldn't talk about Jonah, wouldn't even refer to Jonah.

Except that it wasn't a neighbour. It was Jonah himself.

'You left this in your office,' he said, producing her mobile phone from his pocket as she stared silently at him, desperately rying to conceal her dismay. 'Fiona was panicking in case you didn't have a landline and suddenly discovered you needed to phone somebody and couldn't.'

'That was kind of her,' she murmured. 'Kind of you, too, to volunteer to bring it round.'

He shrugged. 'It was no big deal.'

But it was. He'd driven out of his way just for her and he looked so uncomfortable, as though he half expected her to chew his head off, and as he turned to go she suddenly saw something else. He didn't just look uncomfortable. He also looked tired, and depressed, and frazzled.

'Look, do you want to come in, have something to eat before you go?' she said, before she could stop herself. 'I mean, it's the least I can do,' she added quickly, when his eyes met hers and she saw the surprise in them.

'If you're sure?' he said with a smile she felt all the way down to her toes. 'That would be great.'

She didn't know about great. In fact, she suspected she might just have made the biggest mistake of her life, but having made the offer she could hardly retract it.

'I'm afraid I haven't got anything very exciting to eat,' she said, as she led the way down the hall and into her kitchen. 'Just some chicken left over from yesterday, a bit of quiche and some bacon.'

'I don't suppose you have any eggs to go with that bacon?' he asked, and as his eyes met hers hopefully she began to laugh.

'You want one of my double-decker specials, don't you?'

He grinned. 'I couldn't tell you when I last had one of those.'

She could. Before she and Brian had become an item, Jonah had been a frequent visitor to her flat and she'd made them both fried egg and bacon sandwiches, and they'd talk, and laugh, and put the world to rights, and it had been such fun.

It can be again, her mind insisted. *If you can just keep a lid on your feelings, they'll go away, and everything will be as it was.*

'Do you want me to make the tea and butter the bread while

you do the bacon and eggs?' he said, slipping off his jacket and rolling up his sleeves.

'That would be great,' she replied.

But it wasn't, she realised too late. It wasn't great because he looked so at home in her small kitchen, raiding her bread tin, retrieving plates and cups from her cupboard, making the tea. Like a husband in one of those cosy old domestic sit-coms on the television, but with one very big difference. He also looked as sexy as hell.

Stop it, she told herself as he began buttering the bread and she found her eyes riveted to him. All he is doing is buttering bread. How can buttering bread be sexy?

Quite easily, she thought, if the hands that were doing it were long and lean and gentle. Very easily if the arms above the hand were muscular and dusted with dark hairs that looked soft and silky, and she knew she mustn't ever find out if they felt that way, too.

'Megan Thornton.' Her voice had come in a squeak, and she cleared her throat. 'She did really well, bottle-feeding her son, didn't she?'

'Like a duck to water,' Jonah replied, absent-mindedly licking the butter knife. 'But keep an eye on Adam's weight. If it starts to go down, we'll need to supplement his feeds.'

He'd left a tiny smear of butter on his lip. Just the tiniest, smallest smear, and it would be so easy just to reach up…

'Nell?'

He was staring at her curiously, and she whirled back to the frying pan.

'The eggs and bacon are almost ready,' she said. 'Do you want to eat in here?'

'The sitting room, I think,' he said. 'Like we used to.'

Yes, but that had been then, and this was now, she thought as he bore off the teapot and cups, and she sagged against the cooker. It had been a whole different ball game back then.

And it's a ball game you can play, she told herself as she made their sandwiches then carried them through to the sitting room, to find Jonah already settled on the sofa, his feet propped up on her coffee-table. All she had to do was keep a casual conversation going. How hard could it be?

Impossible, she discovered forty minutes later.

Jonah tried, she had to give him credit for that. He talked about the unit, about the babies, about Gabriel and Maddie coming back from their honeymoon on Sunday. He gave her ample opportunity to contribute to the conversation, and she tried to contribute, but the longer she sat beside him on the sofa the more forced and stilted their conversation became.

It's this sex thing, she realised, feeling her stomach tighten as he stretched to refill his teacup. Before, when we were just friends, I didn't see him as a man, but now… Now, I can't see him as anything else. Now, all I can think about is the breadth of his shoulders, the way his eyes light up when he's enthusiastic about something, the way his lips curve when he smiles, and I wish—I *so* wish—that this had never happened, and I could go back to the way we were, but I can't. No matter how hard I try, I just can't.

'This isn't working, is it?' he said suddenly.

Her eyes shot to his in dismay. Oh, damnation, he *knew*. Somehow he knew what she was thinking, and it was humiliating enough for her to have these feelings about him without him, knowing about them.

'Nonsense.' She lied, all upbeat and positive. 'This is like old times, just like you said.'

'Except that it isn't, is it?' he murmured, his eyes sad. 'In wanting things to be different, I've only succeeded in screwing things up between us big time.'

He had screwed things up? Why in the world did he think *he* had screwed up?

'Of course you haven't,' she protested. 'We're friends, Jonah, good friends, and always will be.'

He stared down at his teacup. 'Nell, do you still love Brian?'

Had she ever?

'We're not talking about me,' she said. 'We're talking about you, and this crazy notion you have that we're not friends any more.'

His mouth twisted into not quite a smile. 'Are we still friends, Nell, are we really?'

'Of course we are,' she insisted. 'You're my pal, my chum, my best mate.'

'I wish the "mate" bit was true,' he said softly, and as she stared back at him she suddenly felt as though all the air had been sucked out of her lungs.

Oh, hell.

Deep breaths, Nell. Take deep breaths. OK, so your heart is thudding like it's about to explode, but don't say anything rash because if you've got this wrong, if you've misunderstood him, you are going to look really, *really* stupid.

'Jonah, I...' She moistened her lips. 'When you say that you wish you were... Do you mean that you wish...that you...that...?'

He put down his teacup. 'Nell, I've always been lousy with words so maybe...' He reached out and cupped her face gently with his hand. 'Maybe this might make it clearer?'

Oh, hell. Oh, double, triple hell. His eyes were dark, and hot, and he wasn't doing anything, simply cupping her cheek gently with his fingers, and she knew he was giving her plenty of time to back away, plenty of time to get to her feet, but she didn't want to back away, and she didn't want to get to her feet.

'Nell?'

So much conveyed in one little word. So much implied, and asked, and understood, and though a niggling little voice whispered at the back of her mind that this was a very bad idea, the hand cupping her cheek was trembling, and she was trembling and she wanted so much to kiss him, to know what it would feel like, so when his lips came slowly towards hers she leant forward to meet them without any hesitation at all.

And his kiss was gentle, so very, very gentle, scarcely a kiss at all, so that when he drew back she instinctively moved closer, wanting more, wanting to taste more of him, and for a frustrating moment he hesitated. And then he placed his hand at the back of her head and kissed her again, and this time the kiss wasn't fleeting but long and deep, sending sensations spiralling like glittering stars down through her body and she arched up to him, parting her lips, and felt the hot touch of his tongue and shuddered with pleasure.

'God, but you are so beautiful,' he said, trailing kisses across her forehead, her throat, his voice strained, uneven as he slid his hands up underneath her baggy sweatshirt to cup her breasts.

'I'm fat,' she said breathlessly, feeling the heat of his fingers burning through her plain white serviceable bra. 'You know how fat I am. You've seen how fat I am.'

'I've seen how gorgeous you are,' he murmured, as he kissed her lips again, and this time his hands loosened the catch of her bra, and when she felt his fingers encircle her bare breasts she groaned with need and longing.

Never had she felt like this before, as though somebody had lit a fire inside her, and as he stroked her breasts with his fingers and told her she was beautiful, desirable, she felt herself begin to float and melt on a sea of molten sensations. She wanted him so much, but it wasn't right because she didn't know *why* she wanted him, but the more he kissed her, the more he touched her, the less she cared about why. She just wanted him. Now.

'Nell...' His voice was ragged, hoarse against her hair, and she could feel his heart thudding against hers, and he was trembling even more, or perhaps she was. 'Nell, I want... You know what I want.'

She wanted it, too, and though part of her still whispered that she shouldn't, that she mustn't, as she gazed into his deep brown eyes she took a shuddering breath and said, 'I want it, too.'

CHAPTER NINE

IT HAD been a dream, Nell told herself as she opened her eyes and stretched her toes, her mind still fuzzy with sleep. A dream just like all the other vivid, Technicolor dreams she'd been having lately about Jonah. But as she snuggled back down under her duvet, hoping to perhaps dream a little more of the same dream, a hand suddenly snaked round her waist. A hand that was large and male. A hand that drew her gently back against a chest that was broad, and muscular, and naked, and she gulped.

Oh.

My.

God.

It hadn't been a dream. It had been real. She had made love with Jonah last night, and it had been like nothing she had ever experienced before, but what the hell did she do now?

She didn't do one-night stands, never had. She'd been with Brian for over a year, had enjoyed a brief relationship with a junior doctor when she'd been a student nurse, but apart from that her sexual experience was a blank, a desert.

Which meant she was in trouble—big trouble—because what did a girl say to a man after a night that hadn't been planned or even remotely expected?

Wow, that was terrific, but I never meant to do it, and it was all a big mistake?

She winced even as she thought it. She couldn't say that. Even if it was true.

Gingerly, she squinted at her bedside clock. Seven o'clock. She was on the afternoon shift that day so she didn't have to get up early, but Jonah did. What if she pretended to be asleep? If she pretended to be asleep Jonah might just slip out of her bed, not wanting to wake her.

'Nell?'

Oh, hell.

He was awake, and he wanted to talk, which meant that not only was she going to have to talk to him but she was also going to have to look at him, and she didn't want to look at him. Didn't want him to see how embarrassed and guilty she felt.

'Nell, I know you're awake.'

OK, OK, I can do this, she thought. I'm a twenty-first century woman, I can do this, and slowly she turned on her pillow only to have to gulp again when she found herself inches away from a pair of deep brown eyes. Eyes that were a little quizzical, a little uncertain.

'That bad, huh?'

'What?' she said in confusion, and a glimmer of a smile appeared on his lips.

'Making love with me last night. It was that bad?'

Of course it hadn't been bad. It had been terrific, sensational, gob-smacking, and, oh, lord, but he had a beautiful chest, and he hadn't shaved it for the night of the concert. He was naturally hairless, and she knew that for certain because there hadn't been a trace of stubble when she'd touched him last night. And she wanted to touch him again, but that really *would* be bad.

'Nell?'

'Of—of course it wasn't bad,' she stammered, suddenly realising she hadn't answered him. 'It was wonderful, you know it was, but…'

'But?' He prompted.

'I just…' She took a deep breath, only to immediately wish she hadn't because the action pushed her breasts right up against his chest, and her traitorous nipples hardened instantly.

He felt them, too, she knew he did, because he suddenly looked a whole lot more wide awake than he had done before.

'Last night,' she said quickly. 'It was just so out of the blue. I mean, I never thought you and I would, that you and I…'

'I know you didn't.' A muscle quivered slightly in his cheek. 'Nell, do you wish you hadn't made love with me?'

Did she, honestly? It had certainly been the best sex she'd ever had. No, that was wrong. It hadn't simply been terrific sex. She'd felt like she was the most beautiful, desirable woman in the world, cherished and adored.

'Nell?'

His eyes were fixed on her, refusing to allow her to look away, and she didn't want to hurt him, but she couldn't pretend that everything was all right—because it wasn't.

'Jonah, what happened last night…' She bit her lip. 'It was just…it all happened so fast.'

'Not enough foreplay, huh?' He smiled, but the smile didn't reach his eyes. In fact, the uncertainty was back there big time.

'There was masses of foreplay,' she said. 'I mean, the foreplay…' Oh, lord, was she really having this conversation with Jonah, with both of them lying naked in her bed, his hip nudging hers and his hand resting on her back? 'It was good, really good,' she continued. 'You pressed all the right buttons. I mean, you seemed to know where…' Her cheeks burned. 'You seemed to know what I would like.'

'But?' he prompted again.

'I need time.' She paused because he'd shifted slightly in the bed, bringing his solid length right up against her, and it was nice, really nice. In fact, it was so nice that— No, absolutely not, she told herself as a dull ache of longing began to form low down in her stomach. Concentrate, Nell. *Concentrate*. 'I…I need time to think this through to…to…'

'See if we can have a future together?'

Yes. No. Oh, hell.

'Something like that,' she muttered, opting for safety in vagueness.

'If it's any help to you, it hasn't been fast for me. I've been in…' He cleared his throat. 'I've been attracted to you for a very long time.'

'You have?' she said in surprise, and he nodded.

'Practically from the first moment we met.'

Her eyes met his. 'I didn't know that.'

'I know you didn't.' His lips creased into a small, rueful smile. 'I don't think you saw me at all.'

'I did,' she insisted, 'Just not as a…a…'

'Lover,' he finished for her. 'I was kind of hoping that perhaps now—after last night—you might—you know—eventually be able to.'

The trouble was, I already do, she thought miserably as she stared at him, but how to explain to him that just the thought of embarking on a relationship with him was enough to make her want to head for the hills? She'd been so sure she'd loved Brian, and yet she couldn't have done, not if she'd leapt into bed with Jonah last night. And what if she was as wrong about Jonah as she'd been about Brian? What if—God, forbid—she woke up in another man's bed in six months' time?

'Jonah.' Unconsciously she shook her head. 'I don't want to get into a relationship with you and then discover it's not based on what I thought it was. We've been friends for so long, and I—' Without warning, tears welled in her throat. 'Jonah, I don't want to hurt you.'

'Oh, Nell—'

'And you must feel the same,' she continued quickly, seeing the concern in his eyes. 'I mean, breaking up with Mary-Anne can't have been easy, and you must want to be certain that what we feel for each other is real, and we're not just two lonely bruised people clinging to each other for comfort.'

A dark tide of colour crept over his cheeks.

'Nell, about Mary-Anne…'

She didn't want to talk about Mary-Anne, didn't even want to think about Jonah's ex-girlfriend, but the girl was clearly uppermost in his mind, and it was understandable.

'What about Mary-Anne?' she said.

'I…' He shook his head, and his voice, when he spoke again was tired, bleak. 'Nell, are you saying you don't want to become involved with me, that you'd rather we stayed just friends?'

Was she? She knew they couldn't go back to simply being friends, not after last night, but did she truly never want to hold him again, or to kiss him again, or to be with him like this again? There had to be some halfway house, some compromise they could make, and suddenly she knew what it was.

'What I'm saying,' she began, 'is that if you truly want us to try to make a go of a relationship, I think we should take it slowly.'

A wave of relief flashed across his face.

'Slow is good for me,' he said, nodding vigorously. 'I don' have a problem with slow.'

'I think we should reverse a bit,' she continued. 'Maybe star again as though we'd just met. We could go out on a few dates get to know one another better.'

'Nell we've known each other for two years. How much better—?' He stopped as he saw her face. 'OK, we'll get to know one another better. We could take in a movie tonight after work then perhaps have dinner tomorrow night—'

'I'm on twelve until eight today, Jonah,' she interrupted 'which means that by the time I get away from the hospital al the movies will have started, and I don't think we should go ou together more than once a week, perhaps just every Saturday, i our shifts coincide.'

'Only once a week?' he said faintly. 'And not until Saturday?'

'Please, Jonah,' she said. 'Humour me.'

He didn't look happy, but he sighed and nodded. 'All right, this Saturday it is.'

'And I also don't think…' she began, then had to stop as she felt her cheeks beginning to burn again. 'I don't think we should do this again for a while.'

'Make love, you mean?' he said, and she felt the blush on her cheeks creep all the way down to her toes.

'Jonah, I need—we need—to give ourselves time so we don't rush into anything on the rebound.'

'Then I don't suppose…' His hand slid slowly up from her waist to cup one of her breasts '…that maybe, possibly, we might, just once more, before we put the brakes on our relationship?'

Oh, yes, she thought as his thumb gently began to stroke her breast and every nerve ending she possessed shrieked, *Yes*. But good sex was all it would be, and though her body might want it—and it did, it did—her head told her to slow this down.

'You have to go to work, Jonah,' she said, trying to ease herself away from him, without success.

'Not for another half-hour,' he murmured huskily.

'But…' Oh, criminy. Oh double, triple, criminy, she thought, as he lowered his head towards her breast, and her nipples tightened instantly. 'A shower and breakfast,' she said, sitting up so fast that his head landed with a thud on her stomach. 'You'll want a shower and some breakfast.'

'Actually, I'd prefer something else a whole lot more,' he said, his voice muffled against her skin, his lips just centimetres away from where they'd been last night with such devastating effect.

'Jonah, please,' she begged, knowing that any second she was going to give in and slide back down in the bed, and he sighed.

'You win.'

She didn't feel as though she'd won as he rolled over and got out of her bed. She felt silly, and stupid, and more than a little frustrated, but one of them had to put the brakes on a situation that was fast running away from them.

'Jonah, I'm sorry,' she said as he made for the door. 'I know you must think I'm—'

'Loopy?' He turned to smile at her. 'You are, completely, but I wouldn't want you any other way.'

And as he walked out of her bedroom, and she heard the sound of the shower being turned on, a smile curved her lips as she slid back under the duvet.

Hot diggety dog, Jonah thought as he strode down the corridor and into the unit, his white coat swinging jauntily. *Hot diggety dog, and halle-bloody-lujah*. He just couldn't stop smiling. All the way over here in the car he'd been grinning from ear to ear, and only the teeming rain, and the fact that Nell would probably have killed him, had prevented him from standing in the hospital car park, punching the air in triumph and yelling to anyone who cared to hear, 'Nell Sutherland and I are finally an item!'

OK, so he didn't much like the idea of taking it slow, and the no-sex rule was just plain dumb, but they'd made love last night and it had been fantastic. More than fantastic. It had been mind-blowing, and wonderful, and...

You still haven't told her about Mary-Anne, a little voice niggled in his head, and he stamped on the voice quickly.

He'd slip it into the conversation today. Somehow he'd manage to bring the conversation round to Mary-Anne, then he'd tell Nell she was his sister, they'd laugh about it, and that would be it. Problem solved—easy-peasy—and as for the future... He began to smile again. From now on there was going to be nothing but good times ahead.

'Beautiful morning, isn't it, Bea?' He beamed as he saw the ward sister hurrying towards him.

'Oh, Jonah, thank God, you're here!' she exclaimed. 'I was just about to phone you. It's Callum Nicolson. He seemed very restless this morning when we did his obs, and when we took his temperature it was way up, and now….' She swallowed hard. 'A faint rash has just appeared on his chest.'

Jonah's bubble of happiness burst in a second. *Oh, God, not that*, he prayed. *Please, God, don't let it be that.*

'Have you transferred him to Isolation?' he asked, following Bea swiftly down the corridor.

'We transferred him as soon as we saw how high his temperature was. Jonah, the rash, do you think it might be—?'

'I won't know anything until I examine him,' he interrupted, but it didn't take him long to confirm what Bea had suspected.

'It's meningococcal septicaemia, for sure,' he said heavily. 'He needs an IV line with glucose, a catheter to record his urine output, and I want him started on antibiotics immediately. We'll take blood samples, but I'm not waiting for the results.'

'What about his parents?' Bea said, and Jonah bit his lip.

He didn't want to worry the couple, but he couldn't keep something like this from them.

'I'll phone them, tell them what's happened. And could you phone Nell, ask her to come in?' he added as Bea turned to go. 'I have a feeling we'll need her.'

They did.

'But, how can this have happened?' Viv said tearfully, as she and her husband sat with Nell in the parents' room. 'He was fine yesterday, and you were saying how I'd soon be able to bottle-feed him myself. How can he have got this meningococcal septicaemia?'

'The honest answer is we don't know,' Nell replied. 'Premature babies, the elderly, anyone with a lowered immune system, they're all at risk of contracting septicaemia, but why some people, some babies contract it and others don't, we just don't know.'

'But—'

'Viv, Callum is getting the best possible care in the world, and if anyone can pull your son through this, Dr Jonah can.'

But as the afternoon wore on, and Callum's condition worsened, even Nell's optimism began to fade.

'We're pumping antibiotics into him like there's no tomorrow, Nell, but it isn't making any difference,' Jonah said impotently, as they stood together in the isolation ward. 'He's still got the rash, which means the bacteria in his blood are continuing to attack the walls of his blood vessels, and now his hands and feet are getting cold.'

Which meant that Callum's circulatory system was beginning to shut down, Nell finished for him silently, and if they couldn't reverse that then his heart, lungs and kidneys would begin to fail.

'At least we're maintaining his blood pressure,' she said, trying to sound positive, 'and that will keep blood flowing into his tissues, keeping them alive.'

'I know, but the antibiotics should be improving his condition by now,' Jonah protested. 'Why isn't he responding to—?'

'Code Blue!' one of the unit nurses suddenly shouted, and for a second neither Nell nor Jonah moved, then pandemonium broke out as everyone rushed to the incubator.

'Epinephrine 10 micrograms per kilo via the IV line,' Jonah shouted. 'Nell, give me constant monitor readouts. Bea, up the oxygen. I'll do chest compressions. Move, people!'

And they did, but it was no use. No amount of chest compressions or the addition of sodium bicarbonate to the IV line in addition to more epinephrine altered the flat line on the heart monitor. Callum had suffered a massive cardiac arrest, and at seven o'clock Jonah pronounced him brain dead.

Slowly the unit staff packed away the equipment they'd been using. None of them wanted to linger at the scene of their failure. None of them wanted to talk, especially Jonah. Nell would have liked to have shared a few words with him before he saw the Nicolsons, but he'd gone before she had the chance.

'I'm glad I'm not in his shoes,' Bea commented, and Nell nodded.

Jonah would break the news to the couple with great compassion, but nothing was going to prevent Viv and her husband's devastation.

Nothing could prevent a pall from hanging over the unit either. They all tried to go on as usual, not wanting to upset the parents of the other babies in the unit, but it was hard. Hard to talk, hard to smile, hard to pretend nothing had happened.

'Have you seen Jonah recently?' Nell asked Bea eventually, and the ward sister shook her head.

'I'm guessing he's dealing with all the forms we have to complete when…well, when something like this happens, and then there will be the authorities to contact, things like that.'

And he was doing it all alone, Nell thought, and she couldn't bear to think of him being alone, so she walked quickly down to his consulting room and knocked on the door. There was no reply, and hesitantly she opened the door to find him sitting at his desk, his head in his hands, and her heart went out to him.

'Jonah…?' she said softly, and when he raised his head she could have wept.

'It's ironic, isn't it?' he murmured. 'All the time I was worrying about Tommy, and it turns out he was just a slow developer, like you said, whereas Callum… I know there's nothing we could have done to stop this happening,' he added as she tried to interrupt, 'and that we gave him the best and fastest possible treatment, but why, Nell, *why*?'

'I don't know,' she said. 'I wish I did, but I don't. There'll have to be a post-mortem, won't there?'

He nodded. 'Viv and her husband don't want one, and I can understand that, but it's the law, and it also might help prevent this happening to another baby in the future.'

'Jonah—'

'You should have finished your shift two hours ago. Why don't you go home?'

'Are you leaving, too?' she asked, and he shook his head.

'I have to see Admin, go through what we did to try to save Callum, and afterwards…I'm better off in the unit. If I keep myself busy, I won't think, and I don't want to think.'

She nodded, but, as she stared down at him she knew she couldn't leave him like this.

'Jonah, I know I said I didn't want to see you again until Saturday, but you need company. Someone to talk to, someone to be with, even if you don't want to talk, so would you like to come round to my place when you're finished?'

He raked his fingers tiredly through his hair. 'It's kind of you to offer, but I wouldn't be very good company.'

'You think I'm expecting you to be full of sparkling wit and repartee?' she protested.

'No, but—'

'Jonah, I could do with the company, too. Viv…' She couldn't finish what she'd been about to say because of the hard lump in her throat. 'I can offer you a lamb casserole with roasted potatoes and vegetables.'

A faint smile appeared on his lips. 'Sounds good.'

'Then you'll come when you're finished here?'

'I'll come.'

He'd been faster than she'd expected, Nell thought as her doorbell rang and she quickly put the heat up under the vegetables and checked the timer on her oven. Hopefully that meant he'd managed to escape from Admin with the minimum of a grilling. It was tough enough losing a baby without him having to then justify the procedures he'd used, the drugs he'd tried in an effort to save Callum.

Give him time to relax, she told herself as she walked down the hall. Don't expect him to want to eat right away. Just let him relax, and talk, or not talk, and then take it from there.

Except that talking, or not talking, swiftly became the last thing on her mind when she opened her front door and saw not Jonah standing on her doorstep but Brian. Brian looking tanned, and fit, and carrying a suitcase.

'Surprise!' he said, enveloping her in a hug.

That had to be the understatement of the year she thought, as he walked past her down the hallway, leaving her staring after him, completely stunned.

'Brian, w-what are you doing here?' she stammered as she hurried after him. 'You're supposed to be in New York, with Candy.'

He threw her a smile.

'I got lonely for you, so I hopped on the first available plane.'

'You got lonely for me?' she said. 'What are—'

'Mmm, something smells good,' he interrupted, sniffing the air appreciatively as he put down his suitcase. 'I'm starving. Jet-lagged, and starving. And I could do with a shower, too.'

'Brian—'

'It is so good to be home, Nell. These last few weeks…' He shook his head. 'It's been anything but fun.'

And did he think she'd been having a barrel of laughs? she thought as he slipped off his jacket and unknotted his tie. She was the one who'd got the 'Dear John' email, the one who'd had to tell everyone their engagement was off, the one who'd spent night after night crying into her pillow.

'Brian, I still don't understand,' she protested. 'How long are you back for? A few days, a week?'

'For good.'

'For good?' she echoed faintly. 'But what about your job—Candy?'

'The job wasn't giving me what I needed, Nell. I was expecting it to be a lot more stretching, and they didn't deliver, so I thought what was the point in staying?'

It occurred to her that the fact that he'd signed a year-long contract, and had now left the New York hospital in the lurch, might have been a very important point, but his arrival had thrown her so completely that she didn't know what she was supposed to think, or feel, and he wasn't giving her time to do either.

'And Candy,' she said. 'What about Candy?'

'Ancient history.'

Candy was ancient history? Candy, whom he described not so very long ago as 'wonderful'. Candy, whose parents hosted all those charitable events he'd needed more dress shirts for. And it was the dress shirts, the shirts she'd dutifully parcelled up and sent off to New York instead of taking a pair of scissors to them, as she'd been sorely tempted to do, that brought her to her senses.

'Aren't you forgetting something major here, Brian?' she exclaimed. 'You dumped me for Candy, and you can't just waltz back into my life as though nothing happened.'

The smile on his lips slipped slightly, and then it returned all bright, and conciliatory, and winning.

'I made a mistake, Nell, I admit that now. Candy was… I guess I got lonely, being so far from home.' He shrugged. 'These things happen.'

'But, Brian—'

'I'll just grab a shower,' he continued, as she heard the timer on her oven begin to ring and her doorbell break out in sympathy.

'Brian, we have to talk.'

He wasn't listening to her—he often hadn't, she remembered—but he had to listen this time. Except the timer in the kitchen was becoming more and more strident, and her doorbell had rung again.

'Shouldn't you see to those?' Brian said. She opened her mouth to argue, and suddenly remembered the vegetables she'd turned the heat up under, and raced into the kitchen.

To her relief they weren't burnt and she turned them down to a simmer, but when she returned to the sitting room Brian wasn't there and the doorbell was still ringing.

Jonah, she realised. It would be Jonah, and at this moment

she could have seen him at the far side of the moon. Her thoughts must have been all too apparent because the smile on his face faded when she opened her front door

'You did ask me to come round, didn't you?' he said uncertainly, and she bit her lip.

'I know, I did,' she said. 'I just…the thing is, something's come up, and—'

'Hey, Jonah, good to see you again, mate.'

Nell winced at the sound of Brian's voice, and she winced even more when she glanced over her shoulder to see her ex-fiancé standing in the centre of the hallway, wearing nothing but a towel carelessly knotted round his waist.

'Brian, for God's sake, go and put some clothes on!' she exclaimed, and to her dismay he grinned.

'I was just going to have a shower. Want to join me?'

Not unless she could hold his head down under the water until he drowned, she thought, seeing Jonah's face set into cold, rigid lines.

'Brian, will you, *please*, go and get dressed?' she said, and he shrugged.

'OK, but when you're done talking with Jonah, I'll be waiting.'

So was Jonah, Nell realised, when Brian padded away and she turned to find his eyes fixed on her.

'Jonah, it's not how it looks,' she said quickly. 'Brian—'

'Is back,' he finished for her flatly. She could see the pain in his eyes and took a step towards him, only to see him shake his head. 'I'm an idiot, aren't I?'

'You're w-what?' she stammered faintly.

'You told me you wanted to make Brian jealous, but I never suspected that after it didn't work with Lawrence, you'd use me instead.'

'Use you?' she said. 'Jonah, are you out of your mind?'

'I think I must have been,' he said grimly, anger replacing the pain in his eyes. 'So, what have you been doing, Nell? Sending cosy emails to Brian, telling him how wonderful you think I am, dropping hints that we might be getting it together?'

'Of course I haven't been emailing him,' she protested. 'I didn't know you were interested in me in that way until last night, I swear I didn't.'

'God, but you're good, Nell,' he said. 'Just the right amount of incredulity mixed with innocence, but nobody uses me, least of all you.'

'Jonah, I haven't been—'

'When I think about how I've been worried for days, trying to work out how to tell you that Mary-Anne's my sister, while all the time you've been playing me for a fool,' he continued. 'I was the patsy, the fall guy, wasn't I? I was—'

'Mary-Anne's your sister?' she interrupted.

'What happened between Candy and Brian?' he continued, as though she hadn't spoken. 'Did she wise up, throw him out?'

'Mary-Anne *is your sister*?'

'Yes, she's my sister,' he said, his cheeks reddening slightly. 'What difference does it make?'

'It makes a difference because you have the *nerve* to stand there and accuse me of using you,' she said, her face white with fury. 'I wasn't the one who kept a bloody great photograph of her on my desk. I wasn't the one who kept prattling on about how wonderful she was, how special—and all the time *she was your sister*?'

'Nell—'

'Was it fun, Jonah, to stand by and watch me make a complete fool of myself when I tried to warn you about Mary-Anne flirting with Lawrence?' she said, trying to sound sarcastic, but unfortunately her voice wobbled. 'Did you and Mary-Anne spend every evening laughing at me?'

'Of course we didn't,' he said.

'When were you going to tell me the truth? Or were you never going to tell me because it was such a good joke? Such a very good joke to laugh at poor old gullible Nell.'

'It wasn't like that,' he protested. 'You're overreacting.'

'*I'm* overreacting?' She gripped her hands together tightly, because she knew if she didn't she would hit him. 'Why did you do it, Jonah? *Why?*'

'Because…' A muscle twitched slightly at the corner of his mouth. 'Because I wanted to make you see that I was more than your friend. That I was also a man.'

A snigger came from the sitting room, and Nell's heart twisted inside her. If Brian thought it was funny then everybody else would, too. Everyone would whisper, *Poor old Nell*, and then they'd laugh, and she couldn't bear the thought of being laughed at, and so she lashed out at Jonah with all the pain she felt inside.

'Jonah, you're not a man!' she exclaimed. 'You're a louse. A lying, manipulative louse.'

'That's pretty rich, coming from somebody who slept with me last night and less than twenty-four hours later is sleeping with somebody else,' he threw back at her.

'And you believe that?' she gasped, incandescent with rage.

'What else am I supposed to believe?' he demanded, and she stepped back from her front door.

'Goodbye, Jonah,' she said, her voice icily cold.

'Nell, wait.'

She didn't wait. She just slammed the door in his face, and then leant against it, trembling. She wanted to burst into tears, to scream at the top of her lungs, to smash something—but not just yet, she thought. She had something else she had to do before she could indulge in any of those luxuries. And Brian had better be dressed, she thought grimly as she marched down the hall and into the sitting room.

He was, and he also had an incredulous expression on his face.

'You slept with Jonah Washington? Hell, Nell, I thought you would have had better—'

'What happened with Candy?' she said, not giving him time to finish.

'It was a mistake, Nell,' he said. 'I told you that.'

'You mean she got tired of you, realised there were other fish in the sea, better fish?'

'Of course she didn't,' he protested. 'I just realised it was you I wanted, you I loved.'

She didn't believe him and, as she stared at him, she suddenly realised something else. He was smiling at her with a smile that once would have set her pulses racing, and yet she felt absolutely nothing at all.

She had never been in love with him, or at least not with the man standing in front of her. She had been so flattered when he'd said he loved her that she'd fallen in love with a man who hadn't existed except in her own imagination. A man who might have possessed Brian's blond hair, and blue eyes, and winning smile, but all the emotions and sensitivity she'd endowed him with had been what she had most wanted to find, not what had actually been there.

'I'd like you to leave, Brian.'

'Leave?' he repeated, then he hitched an I-know-you-really-don't-mean-that smile to his lips. 'You want to hurt me, I can understand that.'

'Brian, I don't want to hurt you,' Nell said wearily. 'I don't care enough about you any more to want to hurt you. I just want you to leave.'

'But we're a couple, a twosome.'

'We stopped being a twosome when you sent me the email about Candy.'

He spread out his arms placatingly. 'Sweetheart, can't you just forgive me, see that I made a mistake?'

'I made one, too,' she said, lifting his suitcase and carrying it to the front door. 'I thought I was in love with you, but I wasn't, and I want you to leave now.'

The incredulous look reappeared on his face. 'Are you telling me you're in love with *Jonah Washington*?'

'I'm not in love with anyone,' she replied. 'In fact, I'm thinking of becoming a nun, or a lesbian, whichever is easiest, because as far as I'm concerned all men are lying, conniving, cheating scumbags.'

'Nell—'

'Out, Brian, or I'll call the police, and I mean it.'

He went, and she walked into her kitchen and lifted the pot of vegetables off the hob.

'Know how you feel,' she told the soggy, overcooked peas as she dumped them in the bin, then switched off the oven.

She supposed she could still eat the lamb casserole, but her appetite had gone. So were the two men in her life. One she'd thought she loved, and the other...

How could he have set her up like that, making her believe that Mary-Anne was his girlfriend, and then accuse her of jumping into bed with Brian just a few hours after she'd made love with him?

Well, she didn't care what he believed, she decided as tears slowly began to trickle down her cheeks. He could roast in hell with Brian for all she cared. All men were liars. Manipulative, scheming, using liars, and she wanted none of them.

CHAPTER TEN

'I SEE no reason to keep David Young with us any longer,' Jonah said, cradling his coffee in his hands as he sat in Nell's small office. 'He's put on weight since he was born, is feeding quite happily from Louise, and nothing about his obs suggests any cause for concern, so I'd like to discharge him this afternoon—unless either of you have any objections?'

'None from me,' Bea said.

'Me neither,' Nell said. 'Although Admin isn't going to be happy about a Saturday discharge.'

'I don't give a damn whether Admin is happy or not,' Jonah said, and Nell sat up straighter in her seat.

'Neither do I,' she replied, her voice every bit as tight as his. 'I'm simply stating a fact.'

'OK, so you've stated it,' Jonah retorted. 'I want David's papers collated and a letter of referral for his GP.'

'I've already collated the papers,' Nell interrupted, 'and asked Fiona to type up the letter. All it requires is a date and your signature.'

'How very…' Jonah's lip curled slightly '…efficient of you.'

'It's my job to be efficient,' Nell replied defensively, and the curl on Jonah's lip became more pronounced.

'But not, I think, to jump to conclusions,' he said, and Nell's eyebrows snapped down.

'And you'd know all about jumping to conclusions, wouldn't you?' she retorted.

'Not nearly as much—'

'Katie Kelly,' Bea interrupted, her voice coming out way too high, as she glanced uncomfortably from Nell to Jonah then back again. 'Mr Brentwood seems very happy with the results of her laser surgery.'

'He is,' Jonah replied, turning to her with a noticeable effort. 'The op won't restore her sight, but he's confident he's arrested any further damage to her retinas, so I think we can consider the treatment a success.'

'Absolutely.' Bea nodded. 'That's good news, isn't it, Nell?' she added, her expression pointed.

'The best,' Nell replied, picking up another file from her desk. 'Tommy Moffat. His weight is up again this week, and he's spending longer off his ventilator. His father hasn't been in to visit him yet, but Helen told me he'll be seeing one of our psychiatrists on Monday, so that sounds promising.'

'It does,' Jonah murmured.

'As Tommy has been progressing so well these last couple of weeks,' Bea said, 'Nell and I were wondering whether he might be able to be transferred to Special next week?'

'Nell was wondering that, was she?' he said, and Nell met his gaze stonily.

'Given how desperate we are for intensive incubators, I assumed—'

'Assumptions can be dangerous things,' Jonah interrupted, a tight smile on his lips and a dangerous sparkle in his eyes, and Nell's chin came up.

'Can't they just?' she said, and Bea let out a small gasp of dismay.

'Jonah. Nell,' she began, 'I really don't think this is the time—'

'Neither do I, Bea,' Jonah said, putting his scarcely touched cup of coffee down on Nell's desk and standing up. 'So, if there's nothing else relating to the unit, I'm going somewhere where the air is sweeter.'

He didn't wait for either of them to reply. He just strode out of Nell's office, letting the door clatter shut behind him, and Nell sat back in her seat and wondered how it was possible to have made love with a man just over three days ago, and yet now long to beat that self same man senseless.

'Nell—'

'Don't say anything, Bea,' Nell interrupted. 'Please, just don't say anything.'

'Well, I'm going to whether you like it or not,' Bea declared, her small face determined. 'I don't know what's happened between you and Jonah, and I don't want to know, but I wish the two of you would sort it out so we can get back to normal.'

'Bea—'

'I know. I know.' The ward sister nodded. 'I'm overstepping the mark big time, but the atmosphere in the unit has been awful these past few days, and it's not good for staff morale or for the parents of our babies.'

I know, Nell thought as she stared across her desk at Bea. I know I've been behaving like a complete and utter bitch recently, but ever since Tuesday night Jonah has either ignored me or treated me like something the cat's dragged in, and I'm not at fault. I wasn't the one who lied—twice. I wasn't the one who jumped to conclusions about Brian, and yet everything about Jonah's attitude, from his icy manner to his barbed comments, implies I'm in the wrong. And I'm damned if I'm going to take it lying down.

'Nell, whatever's upset you, can't you make allowances for him?' Bea said gently, as though she'd read her mind. 'Callum's death hit him hard and I suppose…' The ward sister shot her a speculative glance. 'I guess he must still be hurting after his break-up with Mary-Anne.'

'We're supposed to leave personal stuff at the hospital door, Bea,' Nell retorted. 'It's the first rule of medicine.'

The ward sister smiled slightly. 'And it's a rule that applies to everybody, Nell.'

Dark colour stained Nell's cheeks as the ward sister hurried away. She'd deserved that, but she'd have to be a saint not to have been upset by Jonah's behaviour. And she wasn't a saint.

Maybe you should try talking to him? her mind suggested as she collected the folders on her desk and put them in her in-tray, and unconsciously she shook her head.

Why the hell should she? If he'd made even the slightest attempt to apologise she would have been prepared to listen, but he hadn't. He'd just marched around the unit for the last three days with a face like thunder, and a temper to match.

Well, to hell with him, she thought as she emerged from her office just as Jonah appeared at the end of the corridor and came to an immediate halt when he saw her. She'd spent a year of her life trying to be what Brian had wanted her to be. A year of keeping a lid on her temper, giving in to everything he'd suggested because she hadn't wanted to lose him, and she wasn't going to do it again. Not for a man who had lied to her, a man who had thought the very worst of her.

Jonah gritted his teeth as he watched Nell disappear through the doors leading into Special Care, her back ramrod stiff, her face cold and forbidding. What right had she to look at him like that, as though he was something unpleasant stuck to the sole of her shoe? He hadn't done anything wrong. So he'd lied about his sister, but that was small beer compared to her making love with Brian just hours after she'd made love with him.

His hands clenched into fists, and he swore under his breath. When he'd seen Brian in her hallway he'd wanted to tear him limb from limb. He still wanted to, and he'd do it in a second if he thought it would achieve anything, but it wouldn't.

Well, there were plenty more fish in the sea, he told himself as he strode into his consulting room. Plenty of other women who were just as pretty as Nell, just as much fun, and just as good company.

Except they weren't Nell. Nell, who was a thousand times more fun than any woman he had ever met, and he didn't know what was making him angrier. The fact that she'd slept with Brian, or the fact that, despite everything—he still wanted her, and he let out a low and colourful oath and because swearing wasn't enough—not nearly enough—he slammed his fist hard into the wall beside him.

'Bet that hurt.'

He whirled round to see his sister staring ruefully at him, and managed a smile.

'A bit,' he admitted, rubbing his knuckles, then realised something else. 'What are you doing here?'

'I was at the railway station, booking my train ticket for tomorrow, and it was so wet and miserable out I thought I'd just drop by and say hi.'

He shook his head.

'Mary-Anne, you haven't dropped by to say hi. You've dropped by to continue bitching at me about Nell, and you can save your breath.'

'I just want to know why, having gone to all the trouble of working out a plan to get Nell to notice you, you've suddenly decided you're not interested any more,' she protested. 'Did she react badly to the news that I'm your sister? If she did, I could talk to her.'

'Over my dead body,' he interrupted, with a look that dared her to try it.

Mary-Anne opened her mouth to argue.

'Butt out, sis, I mean it.'

Mary-Anne chewed her lip for a second, then sighed. 'I don't get this, I really don't. You love her, and yet you're behaving like a complete idiot.'

'You don't understand.'

'Then tell me,' his sister said in exasperation.

He would tell her, Jonah decided. Not all of it, of course. Not that the real reason he hadn't come home on Monday night had been because he'd been in bed with Nell instead of the emergency he'd fabricated. He and his sister might be close, but discussing his love life with her would be toe-curling.

'Nell asked me round to her flat on Tuesday night, and Brian…' he clenched his jaw '…was there.'

'So he was there.' Mary-Anne shrugged. 'Maybe he flew in to collect the rest of his clothes, or to apologise for dumping her.'

'Half-naked?'

His sister blinked.

'Oh. Right.' She regrouped quickly. 'Well, maybe it was raining that night, and he couldn't get a cab at the airport, and got soaked. Or maybe,' she continued as Jonah stared at her in patent disbelief, 'he dropped a whole cup of coffee on his pants. Look, did you ask Nell why he was half-naked?'

'Mary-Anne, only somebody with the IQ of a gnat wouldn't be able to figure that one out,' Jonah protested, and his sister shook her head at him.

'In other words, you jumped to conclusions.'

'What other conclusion could I possibly jump to?' he snapped, and Mary-Anne sighed.

'Jonah, do you believe Nell slept with Brian or was about to?'

'Sis, if a bloke is half-naked in a woman's house, it's pretty obvious what's going on.'

'Jonah, do you honestly believe that Nell had just made love with Brian?'

'I…'

Did he, did he truly? When he'd gone round to Nell's flat he'd been stretched tighter than a wire because of Callum's death and when he'd seen Brian wearing nothing but a towel all he'd thought had been that it was Rowan all over again, that he was being made a fool of all over again, and the pain had been unbearable.

'Jonah?'

He might not know much about women, but he did know Nell. She wouldn't have slept with Brian less than twenty-four hours after she'd made love with him. She was too honest, too decent, too upfront to do that.

'No,' he muttered. 'I don't.'

'But you lost your temper, and walked out.'

'Actually, she slammed the door in my face.'

Mary-Anne groaned. 'I don't know who's the biggest idiot here—you or Nell.'

'And I've had enough of this conversation,' he said, taking her by the elbow and steering her out of his consulting room.

'So you're just going to give up, lose Nell, without putting up any kind of a fight?' Mary-Anne said, and Jonah paused.

No, he wasn't going to give up without a fight, he thought grimly. Nell might not want to talk to him right now but she was his, not Brian's, and somehow he was going to make her see that, make her talk to him, make her listen.

Except making somebody listen who wouldn't stand still for more than two minutes at a time and was never alone proved to be considerably harder than he'd imagined.

Sidling up to Megan Thornton in Special Care in the hope of joining Nell, who was giving Megan hints and tips on feeding her son, didn't get him anywhere. Nell immediately left him to it, and what he knew, other than the text-book theory, about bottle-feeding could have been written on a postage stamp.

The afternoon wasn't any better. When Louise Young came in with her husband to collect their son he was convinced he'd be able to snatch a few minutes alone with Nell, but she spent the whole time fussing around David, insisting on taking a photograph of him for the unit cork board, and then promptly disappeared as soon as the couple left.

'You look a bit cheesed off, Doctor,' Tricia Kelly said when he stood in the corner of Intensive Care, fighting to hide his frustration.

'Long week, Tricia,' he said with feeling, as he watched Nell laugh at something Bea had said, only for her laughter to fade when she noticed his eyes on her.

'Tell me about it,' Tricia murmured, and Jonah bit his lip.

He was smarting right now, but Tricia's hurt was considerably more intense, and it was his job to help her.

'Mr Brentwood was very positive about the laser surgery he performed,' he said. 'He's sure he's managed to arrest any further deterioration.'

'Good,' Tricia said without enthusiasm, and Jonah's heart went out to her.

'Tricia, I know it can seem like the end of the world—'

'Doctor, forgive me, but you don't know, not really,' she interrupted. 'Katie isn't your daughter, your child, your baby.'

Tricia's eyes were large and dark in a face that showed all the strain of the last few weeks, and Jonah nodded.

'You're absolutely right, and I apologise,' he said softly. 'It was a stupid thing for me to say. How are you and Rob coping would have been a better question.'

'We're fine, I guess,' Tricia replied. 'We have the occasional weep together about what's happened but, as Mr Brentwood said, maybe some new treatment might become available in the future. And if it doesn't…'

'You and your husband will cope,' Nell said, appearing beside them. 'And so will Katie. She's a fighter if ever I saw one.'

Tricia managed a wobbly smile. 'Rob and I don't feel very much like fighters at the moment, Sister. Road-kill would be more accurate.'

'Tricia, I have a list of organisations that have been set up by parents in the same situation as you are,' Nell said quickly. 'I could give you their leaflets—'

'Thanks, but, no, thanks, Sister,' Tricia said. 'I don't think Rob and I want to sit about with a whole bunch of strangers, crying about all the things Katie won't ever be able to do.'

'Well, for a start, parents of blind children don't sit about crying all the time,' Jonah said. 'Yes, there are times when somebody needs comforting, but the focus is very much on the positive, on being proactive. Where you can buy specialised equipment for blind children, what pitfalls to look out for when your children are ready for school, that sort of thing. I really would recommend you and Rob join one of the groups.'

Tricia didn't look convinced, but neither did she look quite so vehemently opposed to the idea, and Jonah sighed as he watched her walk back to her daughter's incubator.

'All the time we spend caring for the babies in the unit, desperately trying to keep them alive, it's so easy to forget about the parents, isn't it? So easy for us to say to them that we know how they feel, but we don't, do we?'

'Nobody can ever really fully put themselves into somebody else's shoes, but I think...' Nell frowned slightly. 'I think all we can do is to try not to lose our humanity. Our unit is very high-tech, it has to be, but if we can keep reminding ourselves that the babies are human beings, even if they can't articulate their pain and fear, and the parents we meet aren't just the people who gave birth to the babies but people with very real fears and worries, we won't go too far wrong.'

'You're a deep thinker, aren't you?' He smiled, and her face set

'Just because I'm a nurse, and not a specialist registrar like you, it doesn't mean I'm thick,' she said, and his cheeks darkened

'I didn't mean you were stupid,' he protested. 'I meant you have immense sensitivity.'

'Yeah, right,' she muttered, and he stepped a little closer to her

'Nell, what you said about Tommy Moffat...' He thrust his fingers awkwardly through his hair. 'I agree with you. We'll move him into Special next week.'

'Fine.'

'Nell…' Look at me, damm it, he thought as she stared past him at the ward. 'I made a mistake.'

'About what?' she asked, clearly determined not to make it easy for him.

'Brian,' he muttered. 'What I implied about you and him.'

'*Implied?*' she repeated. 'I don't think it was a question of *implying*, do you, Jonah? In fact, it seems to me you were pretty upfront and definite in your opinion.'

He flushed, then glanced over his shoulder. 'Look, could we talk about this somewhere else, somewhere more private?'

'Embarrassed to be seen talking to me now, are you?' she snapped. 'Don't want to be seen in the company of the woman who's the hospital joke.'

'Nobody thinks you're the hospital joke,' he protested. 'Nobody knows about Mary-Anne, or Brian, or us.'

'There is no *us*, Jonah,' she replied. 'There ceased to be an us when you lied to me, when you accused me of sleeping with Brian.'

'I made a mistake, OK?' he snapped back, sounding sharper than he'd intended because he realised he was losing her. 'I'm sorry, all right?'

'And that's it?' she exclaimed, her grey eyes cold. 'Your "I'm sorry" is supposed to make everything all right, is it? Well, pardon me if I'm distinctly underwhelmed. You lied to me, Jonah, and you didn't trust me, and in my book those are pretty big stumbling blocks to a relationship.'

'Nell—'

'My shift's over,' she said, glancing up at the unit clock. 'So is yours, and I want to get home before that sleet turns to proper snow.'

He didn't give a damn if they were snowed in for the duration and, as she turned to go, he put out his hand to stay her.

'Nell, what will it take to make you believe that I'm truly sorry about what happened on Tuesday night?'

She looked at him for a long moment, then shook her head.

'I don't know if there's anything, Jonah. I only know that you'l
have to come up with something a whole lot better and more con
vincing than, "I'm sorry."'

And she walked out of the ward, leaving him staring impo
tently after her.

How the hell could he convince her that he truly was sorry
that he would do anything to get her back? Flowers wouldn'
work—she'd probably toss them straight in his face—and a card
would be feeble and never convey how he felt about her. If he'
had a lot of money he would have hired a plane to drag a banne
across the sky, but he didn't have the money and, anyway, ther
was a limit to how many words you could get on a banner. Ther
had to be something he could do, rather than continually repeat
ing, 'I'm sorry.' But *what*?

Suddenly a smile creased his lips. There was one way. It wa
crazy, and it might not work, but it was worth a try.

'Fine, Nell,' he murmured. 'You want "different"? You'v
got it.'

Nell stared at her television screen, and sighed. Saturday nigh
and she was home watching TV. Not even very good TV, but
mindless game show which was shortly to be followed, accord
ing to her TV guide, by a film she'd seen twice before and ha
thought rubbish the first time.

'Maybe I should join a dating agency,' she said out loud, 'o
put an advertisement in the lonely hearts column of the news
paper. Thirty-two-year-old woman, five feet nine inches tal
dyed hair, grey eyes, has no great expectations of men but ope
to offers.'

Does it matter if Jonah lied to you? her mind whispered
Does it matter if he immediately jumped to the wrong conclu
sion? He's said he's sorry.

'Yeah, right,' she murmured. 'He's sorry he lied, sorry h
didn't believe me, just like Brian is sorry he dumped me fo

Candy and wants us to try again. Well, I'm sorry, too. Sorry that
always seem to end up the patsy, the fall guy, and I'm not doing
t again.'

But what if Jonah is truly sorry? her mind demanded. What
f you're throwing away the best thing that's ever walked into
our life?

'He's not the best thing. He's a lying scumbag,' she told the
elevision, but her words held no conviction, and when she
eard her doorbell ring she was on her feet in seconds, speeding
own the hall.

Common sense told her Jonah would hardly come round to her
at after what she'd said to him, but common sense wasn't at the
orefront of her mind, so when she opened the door and found
Mary-Anne standing on the doorstep, her disappointment, coupled
ith her annoyance at her disappointment, must have been all too
pparent because Mary-Anne stepped forward quickly, as though
he half expected Nell to shut the door in her face.

'I know I'm the last person you probably want to speak to,'
onah's sister said quickly, 'but I really would appreciate it if you
uld give me a few minutes of your time.'

'Mary-Anne, if Jonah's sent you here on his behalf—'

'He hasn't. In fact, he'd kill me if he knew I was here, but…'
he girl smiled a little ruefully. 'Look, can I come in?'

For a second Nell hesitated, then shrugged. 'Suit yourself.'

'Nice place you've got,' Mary-Anne commented, as she
ollowed Nell into her sitting room and Nell switched off the
elevision.

'Mary-Anne, you didn't come halfway across Glasgow to
dmire my décor. What do you want?'

Jonah's sister put her shoulder-bag and car keys down on
ell's coffee-table, and sat down.

'Nell, I know my brother has messed things up between the two
f you big time, but can't you forgive him, move on from this?'

'Why should I forgive him?' Nell protested. 'I'm the injured party here. I'm the one who was lied to not once but twice, the one who wasn't believed when I said Brian had just arrived.'

'And I bet taking the high moral ground is really keeping you warm at night,' Mary-Anne said. 'Look, as far as I can see,' she continued, as Nell tried to interrupt, 'for two years you've seen my brother as nothing more than a nice bloke and a good friend. Then he invents me as his girlfriend, which I knew nothing about, I might add, and suddenly you're attracted to him.'

'That's not the point.'

'It is, you know,' Jonah's sister declared. 'OK, so he lied, but his plan—his stupid, crazy, never-going-to-work plan—actually worked.'

'But—'

'Nell, did it work?'

Somebody in the block of flats had put on an Elvis CD, and Nell wished they'd turn it off. Hearing Elvis singing reminded her of Jonah, and she didn't want to be reminded of Jonah.

'His plan started to work when you saw him doing his Elvis impersonation?' Mary-Anne said softly, her eyes fixed on her, and Nell bit her lip.

'Maybe, perhaps,' she said slowly, 'but—'

'But nothing, Nell, it worked, and now, because of a misplaced sense of pride, or hurt, you're prepared to walk away, to lose him.'

'Mary-Anne—'

'Do you realise how rare what you and Jonah have is?' Jonah's sister said. 'Most people fall in love with somebody first and it's only later they discover they don't actually like that person very much, and that's when the relationship fails. You liked Jonah before you fell in love with him, which means you have a huge advantage over most couples.'

'Who said I was in love with him?' Nell exclaimed, and Mary-Anne smiled.

'Aren't you?' She reached for her car keys. 'I'd better go. It was beginning to snow when I arrived, and I hate driving in snow, but will you think about what I said? I know my brother can be an idiot at times, but he's also something rather unique. A good man.'

'Are you staying in Glasgow much longer?' Nell asked, deliberately changing the conversation and wishing that whoever was playing the Elvis CD would turn it down a bit. Hearing 'Love me Tender' at full blast wasn't exactly what she needed right now.

'Only until tomorrow,' Mary-Anne replied, standing up. 'I hope we meet again some time. I don't suppose it's likely, but you never know.'

'I'd like to meet you again, too,' Nell said, meaning it, but as Jonah's sister passed the sitting-room window she suddenly stopped, and started to laugh.

'Oh, my word!' she exclaimed. 'Nell, come over here. You simply have to see this.'

Curiously, Nell joined Mary-Anne by the window and when she looked out, her jaw dropped.

Jonah was standing on the pavement outside her block of flats wearing the leather trousers and open-necked shirt he'd worn for the talent contest, and it hadn't been an Elvis CD she'd heard but him.

'He must have the backing music on his car CD player,' Mary-Anne continued. She laughed again. 'I've got to hand it to him. That's a pretty romantic way of getting your attention.'

'*Romantic?*' Nell repeated. 'Mary-Anne, I live here. Everybody knows me. It's mortifying—embarrassing—'

'Jonah's the one singing in public,' Mary-Anne interrupted. 'He's the one most likely to be embarrassed, don't you think?'

'But what's he hoping to achieve by pulling a stunt like this, apart from getting arrested?' Nell demanded, and Mary-Anne's lips curved.

'For you to speak to him, maybe?'

'Then he'll have a long wait,' Nell said, closing the curtains with a snap. Mary-Anne sighed.

'It's your life, Nell, your future.' She walked to the door and paused. 'I'll just say one thing. He's going to get pneumonia if he stays out there much longer.'

He would, Nell thought, sneaking a look out of her sitting-room window after Mary-Anne had gone. The snow was getting heavier, and yet he was still there, still singing, looking more and more like Elvis by the minute as the snow soaked his brown hair black.

'He can freeze out there for all I care,' she told nobody in particular.

But what if he kept on singing? What if he was still there an hour from now, getting wetter and wetter, and colder and colder?

'Then that'll be his funeral,' she said under her breath.

Yes, but it takes a lot of guts to do what he's doing.

It did. Her neighbourhood was pretty rough and the local pubs and clubs would start emptying soon. If he was still there when they did….

'Bloody idiot,' she muttered savagely, grabbing her coat and a hat.

She'd go down to him, tell him he was making a public spectacle of himself, and then tell him to go away.

But he didn't look in a rush to go anywhere when she stormed out of her block of flats. In fact, his only concession to her irate appearance was to slightly turn down the volume on his car CD player.

'Jonah, what the hell do you think you're doing?' she demanded, and he grinned.

'You said I had to come up with something better to get you to listen to me, so I hoped this might do the trick.'

'But you're making a complete fool of yourself,' she protested. 'Plus, I refuse to be the one who gets the blame if you catch pneumonia, or if one of my neighbours phones the police and you get arrested for disturbing the peace, so will you, please get in your car and go home?'

'Nope.'

She blinked. 'What do you mean—nope? Jonah, you can't stay out here singing for ever.'

He crossed his arms over his chest in an implacable gesture she knew well.

'I'm going to stay here, and keep on singing,' he declared, 'until you believe that I'm sorry for lying to you, sorry for doubting you, and that I would give anything in the world to take my stupid words back.'

His eyes were dark, liquid, fixed on her. She shivered and it had nothing to do with the snow falling round them.

'All right, I believe you. Now will you go home?' she said, and he shook his head.

'No, because there's something else I want to say.' He reached out and clasped her hands in his own cold, wet ones. 'I love you, Nell Sutherland. I always have, and I always will. I know you don't feel the same way about me,' he added quickly, as she tried to interrupt, 'but I'm prepared to wait for you for as long as it takes.'

'You've always been in love with me?' she said faintly. 'But why didn't you tell me before, say something before?'

He shrugged ruefully. 'Would you have wanted to hear it?'

'I…' She thought about it, then sighed. 'I guess not, but I thought I knew you, you see, and I didn't.'

'And do you know me now?'

His hair was plastered to his forehead in soaking wet strands, and his shirt was covered in snowflakes. She laughed a little shakily.

'Not when you pull stunts like this, I don't.'

'Nell—'

'I don't think anybody can ever know another person completely, Jonah. You might think you know me, but you don't, not really.'

'Nell, all I know is that I want you as I've never wanted any woman before, and as for the rest…' he lifted one of her hands to his lips '…I'd like to spend the rest of my life finding out everything about you.'

'The rest of your life could be a very long time,' she pointed out, and he smiled.

'I sincerely hope it is,' he said, then added, 'Oh, Nell, we're a pair of prize idiots, aren't we?'

'I'm not as big an idiot as you,' she couldn't help but say. 'I wasn't the one who invented a girlfriend, put her photograph on my desk and talked about her non-stop.'

'No, but—'

'And I'm not the one who believed I would jump into bed with Brian the day after I'd slept with you,' she continued, and his smile became rueful.

'Point taken. Only I'm an idiot.'

For a second she said nothing, then she sighed. 'I guess I am an idiot, too, for believing I loved Brian when I know now that I never did.'

'You didn't?' he said, his face lighting up.

'I think I was so bowled over when he said he loved me,' she murmured, 'but I didn't realise that the Brian I loved and the real Brian weren't the same person.'

'So it's unanimous,' he said. 'We're both idiots.'

She laughed. 'I guess so.'

He stared down at her for a moment. 'So, where do we go from here?'

She lifted her shoulders awkwardly. 'I guess that depends on you.'

His hands tightened around hers. 'As I was the one who screwed up most, I think it really depends on you.'

'I always knew you were my best friend,' she said slowly. 'I always knew I liked you, but I never realised why, or how very much. Bea…she said I couldn't see what was under my nose.'

'Did she?'

She nodded. 'There's a song where one of the lines is something like, "Often the one thing that you're looking for is the one thing you can't see."'

'And am I what you're looking for, Nell?'

She gazed up at him, at the face she knew so well, at the man who had been her friend for as long as she'd known him. With Jonah she would never need to pretend. With Jonah she could always be herself, and no matter how many arguments they had, and they would have arguments, he would always be there for her, holding her tight, keeping her safe. She smiled at him.

'If you're not what I'm looking for,' she said, 'I'm in big trouble, because…'

'Because what?' He prompted, his eyes holding hers.

'I love you, Jonah Washington, and I guess I always have.'

'Oh, *Nell*,' he said huskily, and as he wrapped his arms around her, and kissed her, and the snow kept falling, she knew that she'd finally come home.

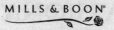

4 FREE

BOOKS AND A SURPRISE GIFT!

We would like to take this opportunity to thank you for reading this Mills & Boon® book by offering you the chance to take FOUR more specially selected titles from the Medical Romance™ series absolutely FREE! We're also making this offer to introduce you to the benefits of the Mills & Boon® Reader Service™—

- ★ **FREE home delivery**
- ★ **FREE gifts and competitions**
- ★ **FREE monthly Newsletter**
- ★ **Exclusive Reader Service offers**
- ★ **Books available before they're in the shops**

Accepting these FREE books and gift places you under no obligation to buy. you may cancel at any time. even after receiving your free shipment. Simply complete your details below and return the entire page to the address below. You don't even need a stamp!

YES! Please send me 4 free Medical Romance books and a surprise gift. I understand that unless you hear from me. I will receive 6 superb new titles every month for just £2.80 each. postage and packing free. I am under no obligation to purchase any books and may cancel my subscription at any time. The free books and gift will be mine to keep in any case.

M7ZED

Ms/Mrs/Miss/Mr .... Initials ....
BLOCK CAPITALS PLEASE

Surname ....

Address ....

....

.... Postcode ....

Send this whole page to:
UK: FREEPOST CN81, Croydon, CR9 3WZ